FAT ANGIE

e. E. Charlton-Trujillo

CANDLEWICK PRESS

This is a work of fiction. Names, characters, places, and incidents are either products of the author's imagination or, if real, are used fictitiously.

First edition 2013

Library of Congress Catalog Card Number 2012942623
ISBN 978-0-7636-6119-9

12 13 14 15 16 17 BVG 10 9 8 7 6 5 4 3 2 1

Printed in Berryville, VA, U.S.A.

This book was typeset in Giovanni.

Candlewick Press
99 Dover Street
Somerville, Massachusetts 02144

visit us at www.candlewick.com

Dedicated to Linda Sanders-Wells
for believing that one big girl had so much potential

There was a girl. Her name was Angie. She was fat.

Chapter ONE

This was the beginning. Angie bit the end of her thumbnail awaiting the result. She had—unwittingly—found a rival. A rival was the last thing she needed halfway into her rerun of freshman year.

That was when Fat Angie challenged Stacy Ann Sloan on the basketball court. Stacy Ann *slapped* Fat Angie across the face. An entire gym class of girls laughed, cheering on the queen of sting, Stacy Ann Sloan, aka the rising star (vixen in disguise) of William Anders High. No one *ever* challenged her on the basketball court, even if they were playing volleyball.

"Say something now, you freak," Stacy Ann said to Fat Angie. "You're crazier than your G.I. Joe sister."

Fat Angie did not like confrontation.

Fat Angie did not like Stacy Ann.

Fat Angie especially did not like confrontation with Stacy Ann.

But Stacy Ann crossed a line when she said Angie's sister was . . . Fat Angie snapped up and yanked Stacy Ann's Farrah Fawcett (original cast member of the 1970s TV show *Charlie's Angels*) retro hair with vicious intent. And before anyone could say, "Damn . . ."

Fat Angie *slapped* Stacy Ann, and to everyone's surprise, knocked her to the floor.

A sudden *"Ooooo,"* and the gym went a hush.

The moment could easily be categorized as un-believable. Had it not been absolutely, unequivocably true.

Fat Angie held up her red, pulsating hand for verification. This was an event she needed proved because the action was too large even for her to believe. She gulped. Her sweaty palm shook and her amazement faded fast because Fat Angie, a mortal among the teen crowd, realized that retaliating on Stacy Ann Sloan meant:

WAR

Fat Angie had become keen on the term. First because of her older sister's fascination with troubles foreign and less domestic. Then later when her parents engaged in war over her and her adopted older brother, Wang, and over who got Lester, the aging family dog, during the divorce. Lester hated his name.

Fat Angie told her therapist, *"Lester hates his name. He won't respond to it."*

The therapist made a note: *Projects feelings of animosity on family dog.*

"Show us your crazy pose, Fat Angie," said a mean girl, her camera phone popping off a mock photo shoot.

Fat Angie did not like photo shoots.

Fat Angie did not like any of the girls in her gym class.

She particularly did not like the mean girl, and she began to sweat and shake.

"This is gonna jet on the net," said a busty girl, moving in with her cell in video mode.

Before the girl could get her juicy close-up, Stacy Ann had returned for Round 2.

Stacy Ann countered Fat Angie's slap with a fierce-naughty punch. Fat Angie held her pudgy arms low, boxer-like, to protect her ribs. Fat Angie, though once an avid viewer of kung fu movies with Wang and their sister, failed to remember Rule #1 in the art of hand-to-hand combat: regardless of the circumstance, always protect one's *head.*

Popped in the face, Fat Angie toppled to the basketball court floor and landed face-first.

"Check out her underwear," said one of the girls.

Fat Angie had had the same underwear since eighth grade — the elastic *stretching* to its edges. She hated her underwear. It came eight to a pack for $6.99 at Wal-Mart and her stomach hung over it. The girls in gym loved that fact. Almost as much as the fact that she was the only girl in their school who had ever had a nervous breakdown.

Fat Angie's therapist had explained it quite slowly and with unnecessary precision. Angie was neither slow nor nervous. She felt the diagnosis was inaccurate and meant only for insurance billing purposes. Her mother had argued at great length with Angie's therapist about the importance of an accurate diagnosis for her group health provider.

Disappointed in her opponent's lack of effort to fight back, Stacy Ann towered over Fat Angie.

"You really are wacko, Fatso," said Stacy Ann.

Fat Angie would agree. People were obese for all sorts of reasons. She'd tell anyone that. If she trusted someone to share such thoughts.

The gym teacher, Coach Linda Laden, who had been otherwise occupied in the equipment room, broke through the circle of ogling girls.

"Who started this?" Coach Laden asked.

"Fat Angie," said a voice in the back.

"Fat Angie," chimed another girl.

"She pulled my hair, Coach Laden," said Stacy Ann.

Coach Laden stared at an aggressive clump at the top of Stacy Ann's silky, perfectly highlighted hair.

"Angie?" said Coach Laden, in her most sensitive but disappointed voice.

Clearly, Laden had a soft spot for Angie. A woman known to be hard as a ten-inch rusty spike had hoped for greater things for Angie, the way she had for Angie's older sister. To see the girl defeated and so unattractively fitted in a two-sizes-too-small HORNETS' NEST T-shirt was nearly more than the coach could bear.

"Angie?" Coach Laden asked again, now squatting to her level.

The girls whispered. Laughed. Angie sat there, her not-so-loved love handles sweat soaked from edge to wide edge of her stomach.

"I have to go to the bathroom," Fat Angie said to Coach Laden.

Coach Laden helped her to her feet. Angie's sneakers, with the sides overturned, slipped and there was yet another burst of laughter from the gaggle.

"Wall sits!" Coach Laden said. "Everyone. Now."

The girls groaned and made for the gymnasium walls. Stacy Ann, however, stood firmly in place, arms crossed, hip angled to one side.

"Coach, she started it," Stacy Ann said. "Everybody knows she's crazy."

Coach Laden leaned in and said, "No matter what, you *know* better. Move!"

Stacy Ann muttered profanities under her breath as Coach Laden walked across the basketball court with Fat Angie.

Fat Angie decided that it must be common after a battle with the meanest, prettiest crank-ho of the school to withdraw quietly into the downstairs girls' locker room. Coach Laden sat with Fat Angie and told the tales of her youth and how she had overcome adversity to become the woman that she was. Fat Angie watched the silver whistle dangle from Coach Laden's chest as she leaned forward, placed a kind hand on Angie's knee, and said a variation of what so many had said since Angie had come home from the institution: "You can't let yourself get drawn into that kind of situation. You're too smart and have too much going for you. Do you believe that?"

Angie had become an expert at the art of the rhetorical question. She simply had to acknowledge it with an answer that concurred with the adult's expectation: nod and/or say yes.

"Come upstairs when you're ready," Coach Laden said.

With the coach now out of the locker room, Fat Angie undressed, pulling her sweaty yellow T-shirt off, the words HORNETS' NEST along the front stretched every which way possible. A cocky, bicep-bulging hornet stared back at her. It had been her sister's shirt. The shirt her sister had worn beneath her basketball jersey on game day for good luck. Not that a girl with her academic and athletic prowess had ever had to rely on such a thing as luck.

The shock waves of her sister snubbing scholarship offers to save the world from the tyranny of terrorism, after seeing a *Dateline* special on the war in Iraq, reverberated throughout the state and beyond. Fat Angie's sister had become a household name, much like Tide. No one could believe that she had joined the air force on her eighteenth birthday and lied to her parents and, most notably, to Fat Angie until a week before leaving for boot camp at Lackland Air Force Base in San Antonio, Texas.

Fat Angie's sister was skinny. The HORNETS' NEST T-shirt barely fit Fat Angie, but she wore it every day to gym.

Wearing that shirt was the one thing about her miserable, predictable life that she did not hate. Because Fat Angie's school day consisted of one or more of the following from her classmates:

Short List
They pantsed her.
They egged her.
They rolled her down a hill at lunch.
They mooed at her.

Longer List
They spit on her food.
They spit on her.
They spit spitballs at her.
They yelled obscenities.
They stole her pens, pencils, and/or highlighters.
They erased her name from school-sponsored events.
They repeatedly lied about her to the press.

Fat Angie skipped showering. She rolled a chalky stick deodorant over her sweaty armpits and sniffed for a smell check. It would do. There were only three and a half hours left in the school day. Three and a half hours and seven months. Give or take a few days for socially awkward holidays and the off chance of a snow day. A snow day in Dryfalls, Ohio, was highly unlikely. Highly, highly unlikely.

Fat Angie struggled to fasten her blue jeans. She stretched out on the bench, held her breath, wiggled, and . . . success! She had triumphed over her jeans once again, despite her couldn't-be-bothered mother. A woman who had vowed during a recent text argument that she would not buy her daughter another pair of pants until she lost twenty-nine pounds. That day, Angie had eaten three doughnuts and two Big Macs. And a small fry. And a Diet Coke. And a Hershey's bar and a bag of Mr. Peanuts. And three Taco Supremes from Taco Bell. And an Andes mint from her mother's nightstand drawer.

Fat Angie had not been hungry.

When Angie dragged herself out of the locker room, the girls were running stands. This was the same as bleachers. Up and down the squeaking steps they huffed. For some reason, the image incited the memory of Fat Angie watching the movie *Carrie* at Halloween.

***Carrie* (1976):** Carrie White (Sissy Spacek) is a teen ostracized by her peers because of her acute shyness and the fact that she freaks out when she starts her period in the gym showers and thinks she is dying.

All the girls throw tampons at her. Carrie later seeks revenge by using her telekinetic powers to flame broil everyone at the prom.

Angie recalled this brief synopsis while watching the girls in her gym class run bleachers. Despite how they treated her, especially when they mocked her in the locker room, she never wanted to have telekinetic powers to destroy them the way Carrie does in the movie. Besides, Angie had already gotten her period and they had never thrown tampons at her.

Coach Laden yelled at the girls, "Faster! Faster!" as Angie walked over to her.

Coach Laden was a very voluptuous woman with slim hips and muscular thighs. Fat Angie wondered what that kind of body felt like when it moved.

"You can sit in study hall until fourth period," said Coach Laden to her.

That was when *she* walked in.

She was the kind of girl who didn't exist in Dryfalls, Ohio. She was 199 percent *wow*!

She crushed the gym floor with her pair of eighteen-eyehole black combat boots. Skull-and-crossbones fishnets swirled up her legs and disappeared at the hem of her red plaid skirt, which was far shorter than the regulated dress code but, based on her stride, she was the kind of girl who could get away with it. Her tattered white button-down with custom-cut sleeves revealed slender arms masked by a soft gray shirt for layering. While it was much too hot for layering, the girl did not drip a bead of sweat. There, in the gymnasium of William Anders High School, was the girl that sound tracks played for whenever she stepped into the room, and Fat Angie was . . . well, moved.

The new girl handed a yellow slip of paper to Coach Laden. "I gotta be here," she said, her chestnut eyes cutting to Fat Angie. "Hey."

And when the new girl said that simple word, she smiled with something no one smiled at Fat Angie with: interest.

Coach Laden said, "Angie's having a hard day," and scooted Angie off the way Mr. Apall did the special-ed kids when they did something on the "special" side.

But Fat Angie could not take her eyes off the slim tall girl standing only a few feet away. The whole moment clicked into slow motion as the girl whipped her hair to the side. The ivory stem that was the nape of her delicate neck revealed a purple heart tattoo. Fat Angie's eyes widened. The new girl grinned at Angie, her elbow in tow by Coach Laden. The coach's gab on mute.

All the obese girl could do was lock in on that grin glowing . . . at her!

Then . . .

Stacy Ann tapped the new girl on the shoulder and the

moment between Fat Angie and the girl severed. Stacy Ann, in an evil Grinch grin, muttered something to the new girl. As the new girl listened to the loose-lipped Stacy Ann, her eyes occasionally cut back to Fat Angie's. Fat Angie's fate was surely sealed. No doubt Stacy Ann would make it her personal mission to enlist the new girl into her army of Fat Angie loathers. She'd get the new girl on day one before Angie ever realized she was supposed to grin back.

"Angie?" said Coach Laden, the mute button released to blaring volume.

The sound of the world returned. Girls' sneakers pounded the bleachers. Gabbing echoed throughout the gym. And the mysterious new girl, led by Stacy Ann, walked away from Angie. Beyond Coach Laden's shoulder, Angie caught Stacy Ann's beautiful blue eyes and wondered how so much evil thrived behind them. Then Stacy Ann's middle finger appropriately shot Fat Angie the rod.

"Remember, Angie," assured Coach Laden. "You are a special girl."

Fat Angie grimaced as she walked out of the gym.

Fat Angie's dad had also said she was a special girl when he'd left the house a few months after her sister had completed basic training. Two pieces of Samsonite luggage and a rollaway waited at the door. He was not interested in the furniture, the extensive Blu-ray collection, or the Superpop popcorn maker that Angie had saved for a month and a half to buy him for his forty-fourth birthday. He merely wanted her to know that she was special, and then carried his things out to the car.

Fat Angie did not like being special.

Fat Angie did not go to study hall after leaving the gym. Instead she went to the vending machine, sank in four quarters, and punched in

173

on the number pad, and out dropped a pack of Little Debbie Swiss Rolls. They were cheaper at the Five 'N' Go Gas two blocks from her house, but a girl had been shot there three and a half weeks earlier and Angie's couldn't-be-bothered mother had been bothered by the incident. She was adamant about Fat Angie not going anywhere near that place. The criminal element could still be lingering, she'd texted.

Tearing open the package with her teeth, Fat Angie considered her couldn't-be-bothered mother's theory and strongly disagreed. No one who shot another person would wait around the Five 'N' Go Gas to be apprehended. It did not fit the logic of the criminal mind. Whereas Wang was of the criminal mind, or so it had seemed since her sister had flown the nest. Even though Wang's court-appointed therapist had assured Fat Angie's mother after a hearing, "Wang is just acting out. He isn't really headed down the wrong path."

Fat Angie's brother began selling pornography ripped from the Internet shortly thereafter and was apprehended by an undercover investigator. Wang was, in fact, headed down the wrong path, Fat Angie was convinced, but she didn't argue this with her mother. Her mother had enough on her plate dating Wang's therapist, supposedly without either one of the kids knowing.

The bell rang. Fat Angie finished off the last bite of the Swiss Roll and disposed of the wrapper in a trash can. Students poured from their classes, filling the breezeway for lunch. Fat Angie hated lunch. Fat Angie hated high school. Most of all, Fat Angie hated that her classmates consistently reminded her of what had happened at the beginning of the school year.

BODY FOUND

had flooded the Internet — the TV cameras, microphones, everyone swooping down. Fat Angie Humpty Dumpty cracked. A pack of razors in her pocket and the song "Free Fallin'" on her iPod. She ran onto the court during a football pep rally with slit wrists and screamed, "We're all killers!" while the high-school band played a boy-band hit.

Images of her meltdown flooded front pages of newspapers and national evening news. Images of the grieving girl. They cheered in parts of Iraq. A victory for their side. They were winning. Only the report about Fat Angie's sister had been false. Her body was not found.

BODY OF SOLDIER WAS NOT FOUND

A guy plowed past Fat Angie.

She held up her wrists, one feebly covered by her dad's

Casio calculator watch and the other adorned by a ratty yellow sweatband. Six vertical scars clawed their way out.

Fat Angie was moving uncomfortably through the crowded breezeway when—

"Hey, hey, hey! It's . . ."—Gary Klein deepened his voice—"Fat Angie!"

Gary had been a bully since preschool. He read at a seventh-grade level.

Gary was a junior.

Fat Angie tried to step around Gary. Gary sidestepped and cut her off.

Fat Angie stepped the other direction. Gary slid that direction too.

"I bet this is the closest you'll get to a dance, Fat Angie," said Gary.

"Can't you pick on a freshman transfer?" she said.

He reached out and pinched her stomach.

She squealed.

Gary reached and pinched her again. This time the pain was deep.

"Quit it," she said.

"Fat Angie the crazy mad cow," said Gary. "Moooo. Come on. *Moo,* freak."

Fat Angie began to crumble in place when—

A charge-shove rammed into Gary's chest. It came out of nowhere. Gary slammed against the wall. The breezeway chatter hushed.

Fat Angie stood stunned to see Gary pressed against the red brick. She was even more stunned when she looked to her right. There he was. All-star-every-sport Jake Fetch.

Kids lingered. The *fight-fight-fight* anticipation ignited in their eyes.

"I'm seriously gonna kick your ass, Jake," said Gary, peeling himself off the wall.

"How seriously? A little or a lot?" said Jake. "That way I can prepare my ass."

Although Fat Angie did not like confrontation, she did like Jake Fetch at that moment until he looked her way and said, "You cool?"

The world had turned upside down. The sky would rain frogs by the end of the day, or at least sometime in the next week, because Jake Fetch had stood up for her.

She ran.

Chapter TWO

During lunch, Fat Angie wrote a letter to her sister.

I am deficient in the art of numbers, Fat Angie wrote.

She had begun the letter during her time at Yellow Ridge, the spa-like treatment facility Fat Angie's mother had stuck her in after the pep rally freak-out. After a nine-day stay, she had been stamped as "cure in progress."

Even though Fat Angie's pre–pep rally freak-out therapist had said to Angie's mother, "Angie's reaction isn't surprising. Your daughter simply feels lost without her sister. And she thinks you don't care."

Fat Angie's couldn't-be-bothered mother, quite bothered by the entire event, felt that her daughter's therapist, a woman she had often referred to as the Hippie with a Harvard Degree, was inept in deciphering the fundamental problem with Angie: that Fat Angie was simply attention seeking.

Consequently, her mother had placed Fat Angie in the care of a new therapist who treated adults. The therapist cost $125 an hour and the office was painted in salmon.

Fat Angie did not like that color.

I'm broke up in parts—fragments—it's not an illness, she wrote. *They say it's "complicated."* She paused, considering the notion of *complicated* at great length . . . approximately 4.5 seconds. Returning to her spiral notebook, she scribbled, *But all things by their very nature are complicated. They are—*

"Hey," said Jake Fetch, launching a head nod while standing at the edge of the table.

The move seemed forced, as if he had spent a significant amount of time practicing it in the mirror but had not gotten it quite right. His white polo was unnecessarily baggy. This puzzled Fat Angie. Jake had a body worth promoting.

"So, you OK?" he asked.

"What do you mean?" she asked, drawing five lines and crossing through them with a sixth.

"Seemed kinda freaked," he said. "Gary Klein's a tool and a half. You know?"

Fat Angie struggled, as any smart outcast would, with the "why" of Jake speaking to her. In kindergarten, Fat Angie had eaten Elmer's glue, nearly choked to death, and been rescued by then-first-grader Jake Fetch, new to her school and already well on his way to the throne of coolness. But except for her near-death experience, the only thing the two had in common was that they lived across the street from each other. Their proximity aside, they were different. Not Romeo-Juliet different. But different in that Jake was a good boy from a good home with both parents and a dog that most likely liked his name: Ryan.

Fat Angie had witnessed the good boy and his good dog playing Frisbee or fetch many times from her evenly square window with a *Pretty in Pink* curtain that only 80s cult star Molly Ringwald could appreciate. Jake and Ryan were an inseparable duo. Just the way Fat Angie and her sister had been. Minus the game of fetch.

Jake dropped his head to the right and rubbed the bottom of his chin. The smallest of scars was etched in the edge of his genetically perfect chin. A chin complete with the right amount of curve and line. "So you don't say a lot much," he stated matter-of-factly.

"That's redundant," she said. "That I don't say a lot much."

In spite of the pockets of kids zeroing in on him, Jake sat across from her.

"You just got docked five superstar social points for sitting here," Fat Angie said.

He picked a French fry off her tray. "You don't really like people much anymore, huh? Your sister wouldn't dig that."

Fat Angie and Jake Fetch did have one other thing in common.

She stopped writing as he fished for another fry. His

eyes cut to her notebook. She closed it with a definite protectiveness and repositioned herself in her seat.

"Angie, I just — look, your sister . . ." and before the stellar handsome Jake Fetch could get out another word, the energy of the cafeteria sparked wildfire.

Over his shoulder the sea of noise and bodies seemed to part. Stepping away from the cashier at the food line was . . . *her.* The new girl from gym class. Her hair pulled to the side just enough to reveal that curvy, unbelievably intriguing purple heart tattoo. Fat Angie, helpless in the tractor beam of the girl's strut, lost all sense of time — space — ability not to stare.

Jake turned in his chair. A fry hung limply from his lips like a snapped cigarette.

The scene was set.

Tables buzzed. Crossing in front of the long-legged beauty, guys cocked their heads for a detailed image for later recollection. Fat Angie pulled at her jeans, uncomfortably camel-toeing her crotch, while the new girl's eyes locked on Fat Angie's as they had in gym. The bombshell smiled and a voice screamed from the depths of the teen: *Smile back!*

As she fought a host of self-loathing thoughts, Fat Angie's crooked lip twitched ever so slightly before forming a dimple in her rosy right cheek. All seemed unspeakably speakable in the mind of Fat Angie. She had reacted beyond the "fat ass, ugly bitch, mad cow" comments. She had smiled!

With an uncertain future but a seemingly happy ending in the midst, all was cut short between the new girl and Fat Angie. The new girl was intercepted. Stacy Ann, also in a red plaid skirt but cut exactly within the William Anders High–regulated dress code, sprung into gossip-girl mode with a coven of three forming a V behind her.

Fat Angie's smile vanished and her head dropped, forming the double chin her mother loathed so much that she had refused to frame Angie's class picture.

"I can't believe you wore that HORNETS' NEST T-shirt," her mother had said, eyeing the photograph. "It makes you look so wide."

Fat Angie kept the 2.5 x 3.5 photograph in her butterfly-adorned Velcro wallet right behind a picture of her sister on graduation night. The whole family, together on the football field. Her sister in the middle, beaming beside a thinner but nevertheless fat Angie.

Jake whipped back around to Fat Angie. "Who's the bomb?"

And right then, a voice said, "You're in my gym class."

Angie lifted her sad eyes, and then they beamed. Jake looked back and forth between the girls as if taking note of the event.

"I'm Jake," he said to the new girl. "And the temporarily mute girl is Angie."

"Hey, Angie," said the girl. "Can I?"

"Can you what?" said Fat Angie.

"Well, the chair is empty," said the girl, holding up a lunch box depicting the Last Supper. Jesus's arms were unusually buff.

What they refer to in the theater as a *beat* occurred.

> **Beat (v.):** a representation of a pause in dialogue. A beat also refers to an event, decision, or discovery that alters the way the protagonist pursues his goal.

Jake nudged the chair leg back with his foot.

"Chivalry. Thanks," said the mystery girl.

"No worries," Jake said.

It suddenly occurred to Fat Angie that the new girl with the soon-to-be-famous intense purple tattoo might have invited herself to meet Jake. The rapid happy-sad-happy-sad confused Fat Angie.

"I miss her a lot," Fat Angie had said to the therapist. *"I feel like I'm the only one who still notices she's not here."*

The therapist had made a note: *Sees herself as a loner.*

The new girl popped the heart-shaped latches on her lunch box plastered with 80s hair band stickers on the bottom.

"So . . . you're new," said Jake.

"In a recycled-high-school-transfer way," said the new girl.

Fat Angie laughed. A half-snort-wedged-into-a-laugh kind of laugh.

"So, where you from?" asked Jake.

"You write for the *Daily Planet* or something?" asked the new girl.

The mood went from light to heavy in a single question. Jake fell into a false smile and stamped the end of his index finger against the table. Fat Angie tugged at her jeans.

"Well, I gotta cut out," said Jake. "See you in seventh."

This stumped Fat Angie, as she and Jake never saw each other in seventh period.

"So," the girl said, "the inevitable awkward not-knowing-a-person moment."

Beat.

"I'm KC." She extended her hand. "KC Romance."

Thrown for a moment, Fat Angie realized this was not an attempt to be eccentric. It sent the oddest warmness into her tummy.

"Angie."

"Yeah, your friend said. So . . . Jake, is it? Jockhead or ultra-even?" asked KC.

Angie stumbled through translating the hip KC slang of *ultra-even*.

"Sorry," KC said. "The Midwest Adjust hasn't kicked into my shop talk. I meant, jock or cool?"

"Um, athlete but ultra, I guess," said Fat Angie, nervously sketching. "He's sort of a shape-shifter. Can fit anywhere. We live on the same block and —"

"Do I detect a little interest?" KC asked.

"It's. No. He and my sister — they, um —"

"Completely tragic," KC said, offering a swig of her low-fat organic milk. "Crushing on your sister's boyfriend. I, of course, have no siblings to end up in such a dilemma. Unless you count my dad's new wife and her two guppy-yuppie heathens, which I don't. Parents. Di-vorced."

"Mine too. Guess we're kinda in common," said Angie, immediately realizing how utterly geeked-out that sounded. "I mean we have something . . . in common."

While Angie was prone to nervous, incoherent jabber, that particular moment was set apart from any other. It was a nails-scratching-on-a-chalkboard, winning-first-place-in-a-relay concoction of nervousness.

KC unwrapped a hearty sandwich worthy of a TV commercial. Cheese. Roast beef, turkey, pastrami. Leafy lettuce, luscious tomato, and the smell of expensive mustard. Fat Angie salivated.

"I know it's a beast. Esther always makes me a ginormous sandwich for every first-day new-school move. Mover's guilt, I guess."

"So. About Stacy Ann," said Fat Angie.

Stacy Ann stared from six tables away. Classic kung fu films would portray this moment with a zoom-in by the camera. Fat Angie had watched such cinematic techniques with Wang before he'd become obsessed with his crime-driven alter ego.

"I'm not so into the rah-rah, in case you didn't figure

from the getup," said KC. "Besides, there's been a Stacy Ann at every school I've been to. Too into chick lit and cruising the mall, maxing out Mommy's credit cards on name-brand purses and overpriced clothing made in sweat factories. What about you?"

"I hate sweat factories."

KC smiled. "I mean, what do you do? For fun? When you're not reforming developing countries' labor laws?"

Fat Angie kicked into the CBS-required five-second delay before asking, "Fun?"

Fat Angie had not considered the notion of fun for some time. She spent most afternoons alone in her bedroom surfing the Internet on the divorce-guilt computer from her dad. Researching the war in Iraq, tickets to Baghdad, and the application process for a passport. All the while, the Weather Channel on mute in the background on the thirteen-inch television she'd bought at a garage sale for fourteen dollars. The screen flickered between channel changes. Occasionally, she propped herself against a pile of overpriced pillows and watched the obligatory pregnant weather woman block part of Texas or California with her profoundly robust tummy. This was the closest she came to fun, but in no way was it worthy of sharing with others.

"Sorry. I didn't mean it to be a showstopper," said KC, returning to her meal.

"No, I just . . . I'm not really the person who's in the know. You know? What I mean is . . . I don't really fun much. But a lot of kids fun—I mean, have fun. Everybody pretty much hangs out at The Backstory. Lattes and open mics. Live band stuff. Mostly garage . . . bands. They have great German appetizer specials on Friday nights and Skewer Saturdays."

"Cool," said KC. "Sort of the Bronze without vampires and demons."

Fat Angie did not follow the trajectory of KC's comment.

"BTVS?" KC said. *"Buffy the Vampire Slayer*? One of the best shows ever. *Entertainment Weekly*'s top 100. A classic but definitely not dated."

"Oh. I'm into the classics too," said Fat Angie, crossing her arms awkwardly over her chest. *"Growing Pains, 7th Heaven . . ."*

KC nodded but showed no signs of genuine interest. *Be ultra-even,* Angie thought, but her concentration splintered. Algebra . . . images of Japan's tsunami . . . the theme song to *Growing Pains* all whipped wildly in her head. Then there was a sound. Laughter. Angie and her sister laughing. Angie remembered—

"Freaks and Geeks," she blurted out.

"Freaks and Geeks is massive fierce!" KC nearly spit out her food. "Cutie James Franco. He's James Dean in the making. Hopefully without the tragic ending. Love *Freaks."*

"Yeah?"

"Absolute ultra, no doubt. The others are way dead. Not that that's bad. My mom owns a season of *Melrose Place,*

I think, and I can't wrong her for a guilty pleasure," said KC. "People need them, you know. But classic old school is still cool. You know, paving the way and all. Like no Lynda Carter *Wonder Woman*, no *Buffy*. And *Wonder Woman* is mid-70s ultra retro."

"Yeah, *Wonder Woman*," said Fat Angie. "The lasso where you have to tell the truth."

"I know, totally beast," said KC.

"And — and the invisible jet," Fat Angie continued.

Blank. Fat Angie drew an unfathomable big blank. She shifted her leg under her, only her jeans were so tight they pinched at the creases of her knee. This was, in fact, an uncomfortable position but one she had committed to. To move again would suggest that she were nervous.

"So," KC said, "when you wanna go?"

"Go?" said Fat Angie.

"To The Backstory," said KC. "Sounds sweet. Foaming coffee and skewer adventure."

"I'm . . . I don't drink. Caffeine. Acid reflux," said Fat Angie.

"Yikes!" said KC. "Me too. But I'm sure they've got water. The nonbubbly kind. Or we could do something else."

Doing something with KC threw Fat Angie for what one might refer to as a loop.

"Why?" asked Fat Angie.

KC paused midbite, a clear indication she did not follow.

"You're new here," said Fat Angie. "There's lots of people . . . in the school. And I'm not really what you'd call in the cool. Not that I don't want friends. I mean . . . It's just . . . I—"

"Listen," said KC, "I saw what Stacy Ann did in gym class. It was beast the way you took her on. Most girls wouldn't take on a Stacy Ann."

"You saw?" said Fat Angie.

"Yeah." KC bit the inside of her full lower lip. "I saw."

Fat Angie had never studied a mouth so closely. She wondered—

"You OK?" said KC.

"Stacy Ann had it coming," said Fat Angie.

KC nodded her head. "So about The Backstory. What do you think? Could be kinda *fun*. Even if you're not all fun-zees."

The Backstory was not simply a teen retreat beneath dim lights with trendy IKEA furniture and a shallow stage. It was the place where Fat Angie's sister had spilled the so-called beans of enlisting in the armed forces. Fried Freudian Mozzarella balls had congealed between the sisters then. All the while, Fat Angie had slumped in her chair and contemplated the universe on a stick, also fried. Deep, deep-fried. She had wanted to vomit. She had—

"Can I? Think, I mean," said Fat Angie. "Not that I don't wanna. I just . . ."

"Sure. Thinking's good," said KC. "Question. You gonna

finish your fries? Kinda like to stick them in the middle of the sandwich."

Fat Angie slid over her tray, and KC Romance ate, like Fat Angie wanted to; savoring the taste of each tantalizing bite. Mixing homemade chocolate chip cookies with the main course, a no-no in Fat Angie's world.

"You gotta try one of these," KC said, holding a cookie out to Angie. "It's massive ultra."

Fat Angie lifted her arm, the sweaty armpit unsticking. The two girls held the cookie in midair. Then laughed.

Fat Angie noticed a stringy scar on the inside of KC's arm.

KC released the cookie. "So, this panda goes into a bar . . ."

Fat Angie smiled. "Yeah."

For a moment, Angie forgot that she was fat. She forgot about Wang's criminal behavior and shady mood with her and her couldn't-be-bothered mother detesting her. A model kind of beauty beneath the bad-girl garb with eyes that matched her last name, KC Romance was not seated at the "rah-rah" crowd table. There she was, defying the gravity of the social chain of Stacy Ann Sloan and the rest of William Anders High, sitting across from Fat Angie.

Then the lunch bell rang.

Chapter THREE

After school, Fat Angie stood at the transportation hell hub, otherwise known as the school bus pickup.

Wang shoved her from behind. "What up, Tubs?" he asked, tearing into a hunk of beef jerky.

A week of in-school suspension (ISS) and nothing had changed. Angie had prayed each night for a metamorphosis in Wang. Even as the dubbed-over cooking show *Iron Chef* seeped from beneath his door while she watched Jake and Ryan play fetch from her window, she had held out hope. But Fat Angie's prayers were often convoluted by notions of her sister's return and staving off her mother's passive-aggressive comments about applying to the reality series *The Biggest Loser*.

Fat Angie hated reality TV. She especially did not like that show.

Wang adjusted his white ball cap splashed in black splats and skulls. His rap style of baggy and bling teetered on the edge of too much.

"Heard you had a throw-down with Stacy Ann," said Wang.

"And?"

"And mom's gonna kick your ass," he said, keeping an eye out for his friends.

"She's still in Phoenix."

"Ahhh . . ." Wang held up his cell.

Her mother was, in fact, not in Phoenix.

Wang squeezed Angie's cheeks. She slapped him away. "Apparently, she's home playing Martha Stewart."

"I didn't get in trouble, so Mom's not gonna know."

"Really?" asked Wang.

"You better not have," warned Fat Angie.

His devilish growing grin signed, sealed, and delivered the answer Angie was most afraid of: her mother knowing she had been acting out.

"Stacy Ann was making fun of her, OK?" said Fat Angie.

"Making fun of Mom?"

"No. *Her.*"

Wang's quiet revealed some inkling of a soul, but he had little room for something as useless as a soul in his current rebellion against all things hopeful. He threw his shoulders back and said, "She was stupid going off all G.I.

Jane and now she's dead. So quit thinking it's all gonna turn out different like your little flashback family shows."

A couple of Wang's dud dude friends fell in beside him.

"You don't have to be like this," Fat Angie said. "I know you miss her too."

"Sell that shit somewhere else, Fatty. People disappear, yo. Roll credits."

Wang high-fived the dud dudes as they all started to strut off.

Fat Angie's breath felt shallow. She wanted to scream. Run through the annoying crowd and scream out all the noise in her head full blare. Just as her lips parted, the intensity of her voice revving, she decided to bypass screaming and go straight to payback.

"Wang," shouted Fat Angie. "Bet your friends don't know you're a big ABBA fan!"

"Shut up, Biggie Sized," said Wang.

"Shut up, ABBA Fan," she said loud enough for dud dude posse to hear.

A dud dude snickered.

Wang rushed her, his face in gag-me range. The stench of Camel filterless, Red Bull, and Andes mints slithered down her throat. Her stomach soured.

"Don't ever say that again," he said.

Her eyes steeled. "ABBA! ABBA! Wang whacks it to ABBA!"

The reason for the building tension between Fat Angie and Wang was as follows:

ABBA (n.): a rock group from the early 1980s; largely regarded as sappy and "gay" music.

Fat Angie grinned, confident she had pinned Wang into a socially sticky corner. One that his criminal status of hacker supreme and karate blue belt could not rescue him from. ABBA was most definitely a roundhouse kick to his manhood.

"Why couldn't *you* just've died?" said Wang.

The high from outing Wang's love of ABBA dropped.

Wang hopped into his cherry-red Jeep Cherokee (a gift to soften the blow of divorce and abandonment). He made a special point to flip off Angie as he cut the wheel, poseur rap blaring.

Angie's sister would not have resorted to outing Wang's love for ABBA. She was the one who got him when other people didn't. She was the fulcrum of their family machine, and in her absence they had not only stopped working, they'd forgotten what working meant. Dad leaving, living in his condo on the West Coast. Fat Angie's couldn't-be-bothered mother pretending she had not needed him the way he had very much needed her. Everyone had failed when said sister-fulcrum was deployed from the United

States into a war none of them could support. Only to have her disappear and suddenly become more visible than ever — on Iraqi television, tied to a chair, blindfolded and bruised. Everyone could see her — feel her — and experience heartbreak for her.

"Hey," said a voice that sounded the way Butter Rum Life Savers tasted.

Fat Angie turned. KC Romance cracked a Coke and the fizz filled Fat Angie's ears.

"You busing it too?" said KC.

"Um, yeah."

"You OK? I mean, as OK as you can be. Best years of our lives, huh? Slap it on a bumper. It's all a bunch of Santa Claus and Easter Bunny, you know?"

Should she have died? Fat Angie wondered. Should she have stayed in the girls' bathroom lighting matches and dropping them in the toilet just as they began to burn her fingertips? All while the school band played the fight song during the pep rally. All while blood drip-dropped into the toilet. All while her sister was —

"Wanna swig?" KC asked.

Fat Angie snapped back into time and place.

"Um, no . . . thanks." Fat Angie adjusted the straps of her overly packed backpack. "You're, riding . . . the bus?"

"Yeah, Esther couldn't get it together to pick me up," said KC.

"Esther . . . ?"

"She's my mom. We've been on a first-name basis since third grade. It's really not that weird."

"I didn't think it was weird," said Fat Angie, who in fact thought it was very weird to refer to your mother by her first name.

KC held up her hand, which had a purple heart surrounding a large black-inked 5 on it. "That's mine. What's yours?"

Fat Angie studied the life lines grooving along KC's palm. All intersected by the thick black 5.

"What's my what?" said Fat Angie.

"Your bus." KC swigged her Coke.

"Two," said Fat Angie.

"Then you get on before me," KC said.

"I guess. I mean, sometimes when they come up from the elementary they get out of order. Sort of that sock-missing-from-the-laundry phenomenon."

The awkward juxtaposition was felt by both girls but covered with polite half-hearted smiles.

"I mean, um . . . your bus might be before mine," Fat Angie said.

KC grinned. This sent a thick gulp down Angie's throat. She adjusted the straps of her overly packed backpack again.

"So, the lunch guy? The two of you really aren't a thing?" asked KC.

Fat Angie was confused. "Jake? No."

"So, he's not checking you out from that eco-friendly car over there?"

Sitting on the hood, Jake seemed to be a part of his jock group, but he was watching Angie. Could he truly be checking her out? It didn't follow the trajectory of her life so far.

Fat Angie's brow furrowed. "He's probably just into you. You're really pretty."

Pretty? Fat Angie's inner-outer spaz had reached painful proportions.

"Thanks. For the pretty," KC said, her finger running along the lip of the Coke can.

"Sure. You know, I mean . . ." Fat Angie said. "You know you're pretty. Everyone knows you're pretty."

"Well, I haven't met *everyone* yet. It's a big world. Besides."

Fat Angie waited for the what came after "besides."

Pause.

Excruciatingly awkward pause.

"I have a deviated septum," Fat Angie said.

The non sequitur was a ridiculous factoid. It was simply all she could think of.

"Yeah? Cool. I broke my nose at a Marilyn Manson concert. See?"

Fat Angie struggled for a response while examining the seemingly flawless slope of KC's nose.

"You see it, right?" said KC.

But Fat Angie's eyes had swung down to that luscious

impossibly possible purple heart tattoo on KC's neck. That was no stick-on from the fifty-cent machine at the IGA grocery.

"Yeah," said Fat Angie. "Musta hurt."

"It did. So critical. I had raccoon eyes. My nose coulda been a landing pad for extraterrestrial aircraft. OK, maybe small spaceships, but seriously, you shoulda seen it. I thought Esther was gonna pass a stone," said KC.

In the nervous bending of her fingers, Fat Angie had unconsciously revealed her scars, peeking out beneath the Casio calculator watchband. KC's attention to them made Fat Angie even more nervous, if that were possible.

"No worries . . . about the etching. Things get dark sometimes," KC said.

The scars burned, itched, and felt embarrassingly alive on Fat Angie's wrist. There was no "cool" about her mother's unbelievable disconnect around the public suicide gone wrong on the basketball court. There was nothing "cool" about the raging hush of the crowd and the band instruments' notes echoing as they fell out of play. There was nothing "cool" about the fact that Fat Angie often wished she had stayed huddled against the toilet in the girls' locker room. Because it hadn't gotten better. Nothing had gotten better.

KC sipped her Coke, staring off at the Dumpster. Graffiti sprawled along one side: **save yourself.**

Pause.

Would the pauses ever end? It felt like a forever pause. And forever could be longer than the calculation of forever times pi—the sum was too large. Fat Angie had officially stunted her hopeful mathematical growth by creating an unsolvable problem. Perhaps she was truly deficient at the art of numbers. Perhaps.

Then . . .

KC leaned into Fat Angie. "Don't you hate it when girls spin all boy crazed? Like that Suzie Kitten over there," said KC, motioning to a short-skirt tease sitting on her boyfriend's slick ride. "It really changes them, you know? I bet she was someone once. Her own someone. Weird, huh? How you can just get all lost in what someone else wants?"

KC leaned away but the smell of her sugary Coca-Cola breath lingered, anesthetizing Angie.

"Looks like you're first," KC said.

"Huh?" Fat Angie said, dazed.

"Your bus. It's here."

In all the commotion of Coca-Cola breath, KC not asking about the suicide tracks, and the simple fact that she was speaking to Fat Angie at all, Fat Angie had failed to notice the line of buses arrive. In perfect numerical order, as luck would have it. Unlike her sister, Fat Angie relied heavily on the possibility of luck. But it was rarely in her favor.

Fat Angie wearily approached the bus.

"Hey," shouted KC.

A guy clipped Fat Angie's shoulder. "Move it, whale," he said, and got on the bus.

KC stepped toward Fat Angie and lifted the girl's sweaty palm. KC, Pilot pen cap pressed between her lips, steadied Fat Angie's trembling hand.

"You cool?" KC said.

"It's a sugar disorder. They're working on it."

KC resumed her attention to Fat Angie's palm. With several hard strokes, KC imprinted a series of numbers.

"Call me," said KC. "Maybe we can do The Backstory thing. When you've thought about it."

The bus driver slammed the horn.

"I gotta . . ." said Fat Angie, motioning toward the bus. "Thank you."

"For?" KC asked.

Fat Angie stumbled on the bus steps. The door swung shut.

The hefty girl made her way through the name-calling, leg-tripping kids to the back of the bus, her eyes fixed on her palm. A heart encompassed a set of seven numbers. She dropped into the sticky last seat and stared out the window. KC had vanished but the imprint of the girl's grin, eighteen-eyehole boots, and purple heart tattoo played in montage repeat in the mind of one unusually tingly Fat Angie.

In that moment of bliss, Fat Angie raised her head to a pair of outcasts she referred to as the Duo of Geekdom.

They should have been lower on the social chain than she was. With their high-end braces and robot-stickered binders, they were, in urban slang, tricked-out freak geeks. The brawn of the group, which wasn't saying much, sported a faded Dolly Parton T-shirt.

Dolly Parton (n.): a famous country singer best known for her incredibly endowed chest and unimaginably slim waist. Her success as Doralee Rhodes in the 1980 smash film *9 to 5* and as Truvy Jones in *Steel Magnolias* (1989) heightened her fame in mainstream cinema.

The ringleader, a redhead with shabby blue highlights, was, in Fat Angie's mind, the brain.

"I heard Stacy Ann Sloan whipped your fat ass in gym," said the brain. "They said you cried like a girl."

The boys laughed. The statement was clearly funny only to them.

Fat Angie had to ride the bus home every day. Her couldn't-be-bothered mother's corporate lawyer lifestyle and not-so-on-the-sly affair with Wang's court-appointed therapist left her little time for after-school pickups.

So she rode the hot, overcrowded bus with kids who were too young to have a car or too loser to score one. Any kid remotely as odd as Fat Angie consciously sat at the front of the bus in the hope that closer proximity to the driver would fend off the anticipated cackling, name-calling, and otherwise unpleasant actions. Not Fat Angie. She wanted to be a daredevil . . . a rebel . . . a girl against the grain, so she rode in the back. The last seat on the right-hand side. In a car, it would be the passenger's side. Fat Angie imagined she always had shotgun — in reverse. She enjoyed the backward perspective on all things. What if ice were warm? What if fire were cold? What if her dad had not suffered a mild stroke while vacationing with his new wife and her son in Mexico? He spoke with only the slightest impediment after speech therapy and assured her when they did get to chat that she was, as always, special.

Fat Angie had told the therapist, *"I don't know why he always says that. That I'm special. Doesn't that seem unusual?"*

The therapist had made a note: *Incapable of forgiving her father.*

The bus came to a stop at Oaklawn Ends, an upper-middle-class suburban cul-de-sac tucked at the edge of Dryfalls. As Fat Angie made her way down the aisle, the Duo of Geekdom shouted, "Fatty Freak!"

Accustomed to the name-calling, she continued to walk, as if ceremoniously stepping off into a better place. Unfortunately, Fat Angie's bland cookie-cutter two-story house nestled in the heart of the cul-de-sac wasn't that place. Wang's Jeep hogged the two-car driveway. She huffed, eyes pinned to the well-worn basketball hoop over the garage. The net remained unswooshed since her sister had left. Fat

Angie dropped her head back, squinting. An airplane flew overhead, eclipsing the sun for a moment.

Only for a moment.

Fat Angie did not like the muted roar of planes.

Fat Angie did not like her neighborhood.

Fat Angie did not like that she disliked so many things lately.

She slipped in the back door and closed it ever so carefully in the hope of avoiding her mother.

"Angie?" called her mother from the kitchen.

A blanket of *uggh* wrapped around the girl. In the last month, Fat Angie had seen her mother for 3.6 hours, and that was a generous estimate. Her mother's way of dealing with Fat Angie was not to deal with her directly. E-mails, text messages, and the occasional voice mail kept them in their out-of-sync connection.

Fat Angie ambled into the kitchen.

"Um . . . thought you were in Phoenix for another week," said Fat Angie.

"They settled. They always settle," said her mother, sorting through stacks of mail. "Which is good because we have to go to your aunt's baby shower Saturday."

Her mother dismissively slid the invitation across the counter to Angie. The card was conservative, like most of Angie's family. Cute in a baby-duck-and-pink-pastel way but refined in font and border.

Fat Angie's mother swiftly slit the tops of envelopes, her technique careful and cruel. Discarding the envelopes' hollow bodies, she moved ruthlessly through the contents. Only a few missives were deemed worthy of further attention.

"Um . . . do you think I could not go to the baby shower?" asked Fat Angie.

Her mother continued sorting the mail. "Why?"

Aside from the uncomfortableness of all gatherings with her mother's side of the family, there was the unbearable expectation to adapt to her mother's idea of normal. Which tended to lean toward being like her triplet cousins who consistently wore new clothes designed to flatter their brittle bodies fueled on energy drinks and eating disorders. Fat Angie was neither brittle nor acquiring new clothes until she dropped twenty-nine pounds exactly.

"I just . . . I thought I'd stay home and do homework and stuff," Fat Angie said.

"It's a couple of hours," said her mother. "You can bear to be normal for a couple of hours, can't you? Besides, your cousins will be there."

Triple Threat confirmed. Fat Angie needed to be soothed. Craving leftover Papa Johns, she opened the refrigerator. She asked, "Where's the food?"

"There's a grilled chicken salad from the airport in the back," said her mother.

"Where's the rest of the food?"

"No one is ever going to love you if you stay fat," said her mother.

The cool air of the refrigerator melted against Fat Angie's fiery flushed cheeks. It had taken less than two minutes for the fat digs to emerge from her mother's mouth. Fat Angie headed for the stairs, but not fast enough.

"I'm not done talking," said her mother. "Another fight."

Wang had no doubt been honest about selling her out. This reaffirmed his position as King of the Jerkfaces.

"I didn't technically start it," Fat Angie said.

"Technically?" asked her mother.

"There's this girl in my gym class," Fat Angie struggled to explain. "She — she was talking about her and — "

"We agreed you would stay on the medication," said her mother, in a calculated deflection of any and all talk of Angie's sister.

"I am," said Fat Angie.

"Then?"

Fat Angie did not like confrontation.

She especially did not like confrontation with her corporate lawyer mother.

"What do you want, Angie? Attention?" asked her mother.

Fat Angie felt her large self begin to shrink. It was an

incredibly uncomfortable feeling. More uncomfortable than her too-tight jeans.

"You get into fights. You skip therapy. They bill us whether you go or not. You understand?"

Angie gripped the railing and made a feeble attempt at straightening her posture.

"You have to start being normal," said her mother. "Give people the chance to forget about . . . I don't even know what to say. Do you know what I'm supposed to say to you?"

Fat Angie's chin doubled in her defeated stance.

"Don't you want to be happy?" asked her mother.

And there it was. The million-and-three-dollar question. Angie honestly did not know. Not in the absolute way that she thought she should know. There was too much pressure for a quick response. Plus, she thought she might have to pee.

"Just go," said her couldn't-be-bothered mother.

Cheeks burning red, Fat Angie trotted up the stairs only to find Wang sitting cross-legged in her room.

"Get out," she said.

"Look, I didn't know she'd be a complete bitch."

"Quit lying."

"You better go to the baby shower or she'll have them up your dose of Paxil—"

"Leave," she said.

But Fat Angie made a fatal error in raising her palm.

The beautifully inked-on numbers were now in clear view of Wang.

"Angie's got a boyfriend."

Wang reached for her hand. She flailed.

"Cut it out," she said.

Wang was more than a stink-breath bomb; he was *The Flash* fast. He snapped onto her wrist, almost making out the numbers when she yanked it back. The ink smeared.

Fat Angie heaved one of those big chest-swelling breaths. Then again. Then —

"Get out or I'll tell Mom you've been masturbating to her Martha Stewart magazines."

"Whatever. Like I care."

"Gross! You really are?" she asked.

"No." He laughed. "But I'd love to see you tell her 'cause then she'd really up your meds."

He peeled out of her room. ABBA's "Dancing Queen" soon swelled from Wang's stolen surround-sound stereo system. Stolen even though he had the money to buy it.

Fat Angie studied her hand. Her predictably miserable existence had in fact become:

1. Less predictable
2. Potentially not as miserable

An equation formed in her number-deficient mind. She reached for a scrap of paper and a mini IKEA pencil.

Less Predictable + Not As Miserable = KC Romance

KC Romance had been inserted into the equation of her life.

OMG!

Fat Angie held up her hand to admire it and to prove the day actually had happened when the most daunting reality set in. Two of the numbers were missing. Smudged from her sweaty palm, two of the numbers had been erased.

Panic panged her. She held her hand as near to the desk lamp as possible without searing her palm. A seven, she thought. The last number was a seven. But she wasn't sure. She was absolutely 99.5 percent unsure. The middle number might have been an eight or a zero—possibly a four depending on how you made out the faded ink. Only the heart had remained fully intact. But the numbers—what she needed the most, should confidence overcome her—had been nervously sweated out of existence.

She yanked open her desk drawer. As she awkwardly twisted her arm, her fingers scraped the underside of the desk for her hidden stash. After a prolonged ripping of duct tape, she emerged relieved with a PayDay candy bar. Surely a PayDay could calm her, comfort her through such a crisis. It could—

No!

She threw the candy on the floor and stomped on it. Again and again, jumping with both feet, shaking the furniture in her room. The flattened caramel peanut goo stuck to her sneaker.

Fat Angie made out all the numbers with the exception of the initial two that had been erased. She held the Post-it she had jotted them down on and bit her thumbnail. The options lay before her: call the coolest girl to ever talk to her or pretend she'd called the coolest girl to ever talk to her. Fat Angie deliberated a long while on this question. Approximately 4.5 seconds, give or take.

She picked up her tricked-out cell phone, a not-so-cleverly conceived bribery tool from her father after the divorce. Angie had scratched out every variation one phone number could be. The total equaled ten variations per number counting zero to nine. Then she scribbled down the total number of calls given that two numbers were missing. The sum total of phone numbers she would have to call, assuming the last set of numbers was correct, would be one hundred. Fat Angie fell back on her bed and examined her palm once more. Regardless of how hard she stared, the two numbers were simply not there.

Fat Angie decided in a swift moment of judgment that it was, in fact, now or never. Do or die. Be . . . well, the point seemed clear.

So, she began to dial. One set of numbers after another.

She was well into hearing "Piss off," "Screw you," and other obscenities when she punched in the ninety-eighth phone number and said, "Um . . . can I speak to KC?"

Fat Angie's fingertip edged for the END button just as the woman on the other end of the line said, "Sure. KC! Your phone!"

And just like that, Fat Angie's life changed.

Chapter FOUR

Fat Angie stood alone. In a corner. Opposite a set of beeping, blasting, monster-growling arcade games. Far from the crowd on the dance floor. Far from the crowd at the counter ordering pretentiously named coffees like James Dean Crashed Why?, How Did This Begin?, and You Talkin' to Me? It was as if she were staring at categories for the Daily Double on *Jeopardy* rather than a menu of what was mostly foam and adrenaline-pumping caffeine.

She searched through the crowded pockets of populars energizing the warehouse-esque setting. Enlarged pages from screenplays and novels, and posters of cinematic legends plastered the ceiling, their edges burned for effect. At the center of the wordtopia was a mural of a 1950s suburban family wearing 3-D glasses and watching a swelling nuclear cloud.

Fat Angie's neck cramped.

She shook the ice in her Where Did You Come From? Italian cream soda, puckering her lips to the straw when—

"Hey, hey, hey . . . it's Fat Angie!"

Gary Klein cleared a path of kids to stand right in front of her. He smelled like Mad Dog 20/20 and herbal tea. Fat Angie inched as close as possible to the wall without literally tiptoeing.

"Fat Angie at The Backstory. Now that's a first," said Gary.

She clenched her teeth. Her teeth should have shattered under the pressure.

"I've been here before, Gary," she said.

Clearly savoring the taunt, he inched closer, leaning more with his crotch than with anything else. "Oh, yeah, when?"

"Just before, OK?" she said. "Leave me alone."

He mocked, "Leave me alone. You know, how do you live with your kind of pathetic?"

Gary scoped out the small crowd gathering around. The semi-OK live band, Tortoise in the Shell, headlined by William Anders High's star quarterback, could not hold their attention. And *everyone* liked looking at Mr. Quarterback. But right then, they were more interested in looking at her. Sort of reality television minus the high-def screen.

"You go," said Gary. "Running out on the gym floor,

during *my* speech. Screaming 'We're all killers, wah-wah-wah. Look at me, I'm bleeding.'" He reached for her wrist. "Come on, show us your cat scratches—"

In a defensive move, she struggled with his meaty grip and pulled loose.

He turned back to the crowd. There was a smell of dissension in the ranks. The sense that maybe Gary had gone too far. Unfortunately, he was too buzzed to catch the shift in sentiment.

"You don't belong here," Gary said to Fat Angie. "You see, the freak show isn't until tomorrow at nine."

Then the impossible happened.

From somewhere deep—very, very deep—traveled a comeback to remember.

"Then I guess you're a day early," said Fat Angie.

The crowd *ooo*'ed in Fat Angie's favor.

"What did you say, *Fat* Angie?" Gary asked.

A hand snapped onto his shoulder. "She said, for the hearing impaired, 'you're a day early.'"

When Gary spun around, Fat Angie saw that her hero was actually a heroine. KC Romance.

Gary sized up KC, still wearing the Catholic school skirt and crossbones-adorned fishnets. Her top tied at the bottom exposed a pierced belly button accessorized with what would now seem to be the KC trademark: a purple heart. Her arms were hidden by a tattered fitted gray tee with a faded peace logo.

"Wow," Gary said, looking back at Fat Angie. "You paying people to pretend to care about you?"

Angie's eyes reluctantly cut to KC Romance. How to recover from such deliberate scrutiny at The Backstory eluded her.

Gary leaned in to KC. His pea-size brain, floating on the Mad Dog 20/20 and You Talkin' to Me? (with an amaretto lemon twist), jumbo-sized his already large ego.

"Wanna get something?" Gary asked KC.

She grinned. "Like a lobotomy for you?"

The crowd *ooo*'ed.

Gary half-laughed, clearly confused, the buzz buzzing off. "What?" he said.

"Forgot. Hearing impaired," said KC. "I'll translate, and slower. You're. Not. My. Type. You'd require a soul or at least a strong collection of mumblecore films."

> **Mumblecore film (n.):** a genre with "a low-key naturalism, low-fi production value and a stream of low-volume chatter often perceived as ineloquence" (*New York Times* 2007). Examples include *Hannah Takes the Stairs* and *Quiet City.*

"Oh, I get it. This is a new-girl thing," Gary cackled, trying to win back the onlookers.

KC stepped closer to Gary. "What is it with you, jock boy? Can't get attention from the pom-pom squad on account of your minuscule"—she held up her pinky—"wienie?"

His comebacks were on a ten-second delay, which allowed KC to continue. "Or is it that you're secretly in love with Angie and can't come to terms with your feelings?"

"Screw you," said Gary. "Dyke!"

KC grinned, tucking a piece of her hair behind her multipierced ear.

"That's all you've got?" KC asked. "An arsenal full of homophobic language and you spin up three amateur-night hate words? Are you really that much of a snore?"

KC had shifted the temperature in the room, and Gary was feeling the heat.

"Come on, Gary," said a guy. "Leave it."

"Watch yourself, freak," Gary warned.

She stage-whispered, "I do all the time."

And just like that, the showdown at The Backstory ended. The onlookers looked toward Mr. Quarterback onstage.

KC turned to Fat Angie, who was still pinned against the wall. Her cup of Where Did You Come From? Italian cream soda sweated against her T-shirt.

"Hey," KC said, approaching Angie.

"Hey," Fat Angie managed to get out.

"Everything crystal?" KC asked.

Fat Angie nodded.

"This is some place, huh?" KC said, taking in the

atmosphere. "You wouldn't tell it from the outside. Looks kinda 80s pop, you know?"

Fat Angie actually did know, and she grinned while KC whipped out her cell phone. Clicking to camera mode, KC snapped a picture of the ceiling.

"Check it out," KC said, leaning in closer than anyone who didn't want to eviscerate Fat Angie had in the last few months. "Sweet, huh? I'm totally sticking that on my Wall of Thoughts So Twisted." KC hovered the camera slightly above them and moved in for a "say cheese" moment.

"I'm — the camera thing," said Fat Angie.

"It'll be a quickie," said KC.

Fat Angie fell heart-forward into KC's dark eyes. "'K," said Fat Angie.

The camera phone flash-snapped. Fat Angie's eyes were closed.

"That would be good for your Wall of Weird and Twisted," said Fat Angie.

KC saved the photo.

"Yeah, not so much," KC said. "Closing your eyes is pretty normal. The Wall of Thoughts So Twisted is plastered with articles like 'Cheerleader Caves under Cambodian Web Scandal.' Or a photo of JFK holding Jimi Hendrix on his shoulders and Jimi holding the world on his. Or a headline like 'Playwright Preverbal Play Plops: Pounces Pumice Onstage.'"

"Um, that's pretty —"

"Twisted?" asked KC.

"Yeah."

"It kind of reminds me that the world can be a lot stranger than my everyday life."

Pause.

Tortoise in the Shell started a new song.

"They're pretty good — the band," KC said. "Kinda Iron and Wine and the Kills sandwiched with a little Doors."

"Yeah. They sell T-shirts."

"Yeah?"

"Yup," said Fat Angie, her mind racing for a more interesting topic.

"So . . ." KC said.

A "so" was never a good starting point for Fat Angie. It led to uncomfortable pauses that made her armpits sweat.

Fat Angie nodded her head.

Pause.

Pause. The dreadful "so" pause.

"What's your mix?" said KC, killing the weirdness. "Your drink?"

"Um . . ."

Fat Angie had mastered the "um" shortly after her alleged nervous breakdown. It filled the space to make doctors — and, most important, her couldn't-be-bothered mother — feel that something more and hopeful would blossom from her lips. However, that was a rare phenomenon . . . like a quality hit show for the teen bracket on CBS.

Fat Angie's eyes pinned on to Gary sneering from the pool table. KC followed the look.

"You scared of him?" said KC. "I mean, is that why you're so —"

"Um . . . no," Fat Angie said. "He's just . . ."

"An asshole?"

Fat Angie rarely communicated using profanities. To be more specific, she never did. Her mother said it was a language of ignorance and poverty. Fat Angie was neither ignorant nor poor, according to her standardized tests and her mother's income tax return.

"You know, Angie, they got one of those guys in every school I've been to."

"How many would that be exactly?" asked Fat Angie.

KC grinned. "I don't know exactly."

Fat Angie smiled. She had no idea what propelled this reaction. It was a soft smile. An unpracticed one. It was . . . real?

KC's smile widened. They were in the middle of their smilefest when Jake stepped in, throwing his head back in that awkward, overly practiced way.

"Hey," he said.

Smilefest ended.

"Oh," said Fat Angie. "Hey. Jake."

KC executed a perfected pretend grin combined with a raised, pierced eyebrow. "What up, Jack?"

"Jake," he said, correcting her.

"I know," said KC. "Esther, my mom, she says that to all her clients. Her catchphrases are kinda habit-forming."

Sucking on her straw, Fat Angie said, "What exactly does your mother do?"

"She's into tats mostly. Tattoos? Why? What do your parents do?"

Fat Angie nervously sipped her Where Did You Come From? Italian cream soda. *Be absolutely cool,* she thought. Her mind raced. What did her mother do? Besides reign humiliation on Angie and any client fool enough to tangle with her? The Backstory shifted in disjointed photo time lapse. "My mom's a . . . a criminal."

Jake did a double take.

"Yeah," said Fat Angie. "Real hard-core."

"Really?" said KC, suspicious.

"No," said Jake. "Her mom's a corporate lawyer."

"Same thing," Fat Angie said.

"It's nothing to be embarrassed about," said Jake. "My parents are accountants." Jake snagged Fat Angie's drink from her.

His lips met the straw before she could stop him.

"Wow," said KC. "So, you guys are all 'burbing it, huh? Minivans and listening to underground rap from the early 90s."

"Don't you think that's kind of a stereotype?" Jake said.

"Oh," KC said, smiling mockingly. "My bad."

"Almost everyone has to drive at least twenty miles to work," Jake said in a passive-aggressive tone. "Dryfalls, Ohio, is not exactly a Starbucks town. I mean, it's not like our zip code is ripped off a TV show or anything."

"OK, what's really itching you, Jack?" KC asked.

"Jake. My name is Jake. It's probably too bland for you, California."

Fat Angie did not follow the trajectory of the conversation, as it was second-level dialogue.

Second-level dialogue (n.): dialogue in which the speaker says one thing but means another.

"Still scooping for the *Daily Planet*?" said KC. "Big superjock *S* on your chest?"

Fat Angie did not like confrontation.

Fat Angie especially did not like *this* confrontation.

Why were Jake and KC in a head-to-head battle using second-level dialogue and Superman references? While athletic, he clearly did not have the comic-book hero's build.

"It doesn't take much to find something if your name's KC Romance," said Jake.

"You Scoobied me?" said KC. "I met you, like, what, eight hours ago?"

Fat Angie said, "You Scoobied her?" Then she leaned in

to Jake. "What *exactly* is Scoobied, and is that OK for you to do?"

"According to your online yearbook, you useta be a regular Stacy Ann in Beverly Hills," Jake said.

"Read the fine print, Clark Kent," said KC. "I'm nothing like Stacy Ann."

"Jake." Fat Angie pulled him away from KC. "Seriously. We don't talk. Now you're bullying the only person who has *willingly* talked to me in forever."

"Come on, people talk to you," Jake said.

"No, they don't."

"Melissa Peel? Rosie Hernandez?"

Fat Angie glared. These people talked *at* her. Looking behind her. They talked to anyone who would listen.

"Even so," Jake said, "KC is not like you. Just trust me, OK?"

"I don't, OK?"

"Your sister—" Jake stopped himself midsentence.

"What?" Fat Angie asked.

Jake was a good boy from a good home that, as far as Fat Angie could tell, had little conflict. While he had played one-on-one games in their driveway with her sister, Jake and Fat Angie had rarely spoken. Standing in The Backstory, Fat Angie began to wonder why. Just as the question took shape Jake said, "Look, I checked out her Facebook. KC's got history. A lot of history."

"So what?" she asked. "And why do you care?"

Jake nodded ever so slightly. Fat Angie often lacked the skill of nonverbal communication. She felt the weight of her disability quite distinctively at that moment.

"Look, I just do," Jake said.

Fat Angie looked over her shoulder. KC stood, her boots pigeon-toed. Fat Angie turned back to Jake. The equation of the moment was too complicated. She was terrible with numbers, her mother consistently reminded her. She was nothing like her sister. She was nothing. Tortoise in the Shell jamming, the villains dropping dead in the shoot-'em-up video game, and the smell of giant peanut-butter cups overwhelmed her.

"I gotta go," Fat Angie said to Jake.

Jake cracked his neck, the sound painfully audible, and strutted out the door.

"Hey," Fat Angie said to KC.

"Moment of awkward, huh?"

"Guess."

"So, the Stacy Ann thing—back in the Hills," said KC. "He's not a hundred percent off and not a hundred percent on. It was just a different . . . crowd. Kinda."

"I don't care," said Fat Angie. "I mean, unless you're plotting to destroy my life."

"Not likely."

Sheepish smilefest back on.

"So, what are you drinking?" KC asked Fat Angie.

Fat Angie held the cup out for KC, who, upon taking

it, touched Fat Angie's hand. This sent Fat Angie into what some refer to as a maximum sensory overload. Butterflies swarmed in her stomach and mishmashed with the recently ingested concoction of soda and half-and-half. The girls' exchange had a staying power foreign to Fat Angie.

Then.

Straw. Lips. KC's eyes lifted. Angie's heart seemed to split. That something that told Fat Angie to smile earlier in the cafeteria that day said, *Speak, you freak! Speak! Say . . .*

"I think you rock," Fat Angie blurted out, unsure exactly what she meant.

The moment was stellar odd, complete with racing pulse accessories in the geekness of Fat Angie.

"I mean . . . um . . . I think . . ." continued Fat Angie. "Um, that you are . . . um . . . swell."

Swell? Of all the words in the modern English language, including slang, Fat Angie had resorted to a 1950s *Leave It to Beaver* "swell." The passion behind the word faded as she realized what had actually stepped out of her mouth.

KC's expression held unreadable. Mad, sad, glad . . . hands down, she had mastered the poker face.

"Swell," KC repeated. "Cool . . . I've never been a swell."

"Yeah?"

KC nodded. Fat Angie nodded. So began a nodfest.

"You wanna go get some pancakes at an IHOP?" said KC. "I'm raging hungry."

"Dryfalls is kinda a Waffle House town," said Fat Angie.

"Way too truck stop," KC said.

"The Kick You Like a Legend chicken-salad wrap is award-winning," said Fat Angie, motioning toward the counter. "Picked Best Wrap in four counties."

"Split one?" KC asked.

"Definitely."

Just like that, KC Romance and Fat Angie walked side by side through the smell of lattes and pounding booming bass. There seemed nothing more normal in the world to Angie at that moment and she had no idea why.

Chapter FIVE

Fat Angie had slept approximately four hours and fifty-two minutes after returning from The Backstory. As kids pushed past her in the hallway, all she could think of was KC's grin the night before and that enticing purple heart tattooed on the side of her neck. So engrossed was she in the recollection that she nearly failed to see the tattoo come into full view as KC turned the corner. Fat Angie quickly rubbed sleepy crust from her eyes. The crusty flakes clung to her T-shirt. KC's grin speared through the crowd and landed in the rapidly pumping heart of Fat Angie. The moment. It was *swell . . . ing*.

Butterflies-in-belly fluttered. It was as if the crowd of chattering, texting kids parted like the Red Sea for the sexy Ms. Romance. Stacy Ann Sloan took note of this phenomenon, mostly because the stocky jock she was talking to craned his neck to catch a glimpse of the Amazon beauty runwaying it like New York Fashion Week.

Fat Angie smiled.

She adjusted her backpack straps.

She tugged at her slightly too-tight T-shirt.

She gulped.

She leaned against the lockers with her right shoulder. That was awkward.

She stood with her weight evenly distributed.

She suddenly wished she had peed.

"Hey," said KC, sipping something steamy from a tattoo convention travel mug. "Get any crash time?"

"Not really."

"I'm not real big on the sleep gig," said KC. "You can sleep when you die, right?"

The morbidity of the statement made Fat Angie uncomfortable to the nth degree.

PRESUMED DEAD

had been the headline on one website covering her sister's disappearance. A video stream with Iraqi script along the bottom and top. Her sister seated at center for the whole world to see. Beaten, bruised, and forced to spit out a scripted plea for the release of Iraqi war prisoners. Beneath the dirt and blood, beneath the scripted plea to the world, her sister seemingly fearless. Even with a gun pressed to her sweaty temple. Fat Angie had downloaded the forty-five-second video and kept it in her desktop folder marked FAMILY PICS.

"What?" KC said.

"Nothing," said Fat Angie.

"Doesn't seem like a no-thing," said KC.

Fat Angie fidgeted with her locker handle.

"Something you wanna tell me?" said KC, almost seeming to bait her.

"Um . . . no," Fat Angie said.

KC dug around her tattered black messenger bag covered with underground rock band patches and political pins. Fat Angie noticed one pin with the peace sign in silhouette and a background of rainbow colors descending top to bottom.

KC held out a square-folded note with a purple heart colored in scented marker on the front.

"You wrote me a note?" Fat Angie asked.

"Guess I could've texted, but I'm old-school. Yeah, I wrote you a note. Think of it as the scratchings of a deranged young woman."

No one had ever given Fat Angie a note, though many notes *about* her had been passed from desk to desk. Drawings with Fat Angie's head on a pig's body. Her feet as pig hooves. In one such note, her head from an eighth-grade class photo was taped on the body of Jabba the Hutt.

So a note *for* Fat Angie had become a rather impossible possibility, but there it was, resting softly in her palm. This was significant and required an immediate response. Fat

Angie did not always do well at immediate responses. It was something the doctors at Yellow Ridge had diagnosed as post-traumatic stress disorder (PTSD).

Post-traumatic stress disorder (n): a psychiatric condition that can develop following any traumatic, catastrophic life experience.

The PTSD diagnosis infuriated Fat Angie's couldn't-be-bothered mother. She felt Fat Angie would use the diagnosis as an all-access pass to continue to behave "unusually."

Rather than reading the note, Fat Angie feverishly dug into her backpack. After accidentally dumping the contents on the floor, she sifted through wads of college-ruled notebook paper, a series of pen caps, an unwrapped tampon, and a stick of Black Jack gum. She found her gem wedged between her science and history books.

"Here," Fat Angie said, dangling a LIVESTRONG bracelet from her fingertips.

KC knelt.

"It's not as cool as a note," said Fat Angie. "But, um . . ."

"No, I'm with the ixnay on cancer."

KC slipped off her Che sweatband and, as with a Cinderella slipper for the wrist, slid on the yellow bracelet.

She held up her arm to Fat Angie. "What do you think?"

Fat Angie had never given anything to anyone without a special occasion — well, except to her sister. "Cool . . ."

KC picked up the piece of Black Jack gum and slipped the stick in her mouth, drawing further attention to her lips.

The warning bell buzzed.

"We better fly," said KC.

Fat Angie restuffed her backpack. Stacy Ann Sloan glared as she walked past them.

"She really is a vicious bitch, isn't she?" said KC.

Fat Angie adjusted her backpack straps. "You should meet my brother."

The girls walked down the hall.

"You know what I don't like about girls like Stacy Ann?" said KC. "Their innate ability to humiliate any and everyone, with no conscience. They're just too scared to be who they really are," said KC.

"She comes from a long line of fearless brothers and sisters. Her dad is like a supermarine or something. I don't think she's scared of anything," said Fat Angie.

"Yeah, she is. She's scared to death," said KC. "Not like you."

"I'm scared all the time," said Fat Angie, unsure why she had just divulged such privileged information.

KC stopped in the middle of the hallway. Kids cut around them, between them.

Pause.

"I'll see you at lunch," KC said.

"Sure," said Fat Angie. "See ya."

Fat Angie stood at what could be described as a

crossroads, if the halls were in fact roads, feeling so . . . STUPID! *I'm scared all the time,* she thought. That was beyond stupid. Fat Angie lowered her head and huffed to class. Her incredibly tight jeans felt tighter and tighter.

After stumbling around a corner, Fat Angie's sneakers squeaked to a fast stop. Mid-hallway, Stacy Ann Sloan's posse hung behind their queen in classic V duck-flight formation as the perfectly assembled girl bent over at the water fountain. When she straightened, the first thing she saw was Fat Angie. A drop of water clung to Stacy Ann's vivacious rosemary lipstick.

"Why?" asked Stacy Ann, strutting toward the fat girl.

"Why what?" Fat Angie asked.

"Why are you walking down the same hallway as me?" Stacy Ann asked.

The answer was blatantly obvious to Fat Angie. The only alternative route would require her to run two flights downstairs, take three hall turns, and trudge two flights up again. That seemed excessive avoidance of any single person or thing. Unless the thing had fourteen heads, seven clawed hands, and a single eye. *Then again, was there really much of a difference?* Fat Angie thought.

"Well?" said Stacy Ann.

Fat Angie stepped around Stacy Ann and her ominous posse, when Stacy Ann grabbed the back of Fat Angie's hair.

"Squeal, wacko," commanded Stacy Ann.

That phrase was not foreign to Fat Angie. She had

endured some variation of it, with the occasional tummy poke or oink sound, for some time. However, Stacy Ann's direct command while holding Fat Angie's hair threaded between her fingers brought the girl to her knees, a position of submission she had never assumed for anyone.

"Squeal," Stacy Ann said, twisting Fat Angie's unkempt hair.

Fat Angie's resistance only increased the sting-ouch pain penetrating her scalp.

"Squeal," Stacy Ann demanded.

Then Fat Angie let out, however faintly, a squeal.

"Louder," said Stacy Ann.

Fat Angie's body shook. It sweated. Tears welled in her eyes though none fell.

The posse giggled. They snickered. Their lip gloss glowed a muted red-green beneath the fluorescent hallway lights. What a vicious group of vixens they were. Even if one of them was the vice president of the Christians Against a Violent Society (CAVS). Clearly, she was not suited for that office.

Then the tardy bell buzzed.

"Shit," said one of the posse. "We gotta go, Stacy Ann."

"Mrs. Ermis will cut us slack," said Stacy Ann. "Besides"—the girl's grip twisted even tighter—"Fat Angie hasn't squealed loud enough yet."

Fat Angie's jaw fell open. She panted in pain. Her head throbbed.

"Squeal louder," ordered Stacy Ann, yanking Fat Angie to the floor.

Whether it was fate — or simply a teacher stepping out to urinate during his off period — the universe intervened.

"Hey," said the teacher. "What's going on there?"

Stacy Ann's jaws-of-life grip loosened and the four of them smiled innocently.

"She fell," said Stacy Ann. "We were trying to help her."

The girls attempted to help Fat Angie to her feet but she flung loose like a crazy thing.

"It's Angie," said Stacy Ann. "The girl from the pep rally."

The teacher stepped toward them.

"Oh. Yeah," he said.

Stacy Ann leaned in to Fat Angie. "You say anything, pig, and I'll kick your ass every day for the rest of the year."

The teacher helped Fat Angie to her feet. "The rest of you get to class.

"You OK?" the teacher asked.

"Um," said Fat Angie, massaging her head.

She wanted to rat out Stacy Ann. Describe every hair-pulling detail, leaving not one single agonizing moment of the humiliating experience to the imagination.

But she said nothing to implicate the rising pride of William Anders High — the honor-roll-listed, up-and-coming athletic queen. The girl most envied for playing the good, the bad, and the beautiful and still managing to seem like a fully fleshed-out character in a well-thought-out novel. Stacy Ann Sloan was scared of nothing. That much Fat Angie believed.

Fat Angie stood awkwardly, tugging at the inner thighs of her jeans to release a very uncomfortable pinching.

"You sure you're all right?" said the teacher.

"I'm late. . . . Can you get me a pass or something?" said Fat Angie.

"Sure," he said, rubbing the back of his neck. "Let's go."

The two walked side by side, but Fat Angie was clearly walking alone.

Fat Angie eyed her Casio calculator watch. There were only five minutes left in lunch period. She saw Jake at a table of whiz-kid smart jocks. She saw Stacy Ann Sloan with the goodie-baddies. She saw the world of William Anders High in its pockets of cloistered peeps. And she sat sequestered from them with a trough of yuck in front of her. And no KC.

She slid the tray to the side and flipped open her spiral notebook to the ongoing letter to her sister.

She wrote: *Today I stood up to Stacy Ann Sloan. You would've loved it!*

Fat Angie stared down at the two false statements, the exclamation point pointing to no real excitement. She had cowered—she had caved. She had been nothing like her sister. She had been nothing but the "special" fat girl who'd squealed for Stacy Ann Sloan.

Beat.

Maybe that was what had kept the tough-cool KC Romance out of the cafeteria. Maybe she had heard—maybe everyone knew. Fat Angie surveyed the cafeteria with a more defined paranoia. She slammed her spiral notebook closed and dumped out her tray. Looking over her shoulder as she pushed through the glass double doors, she saw Stacy Ann sneering at her. Of course, everyone knew. Fat Angie could hide nothing.

After school, Fat Angie sat on a railing with the school bus brigade. It was an unpleasant ritual that only counting in her head could get her through. Until—

"Hey," said KC from behind her.

Fat Angie stood. "Hey."

"Sorry about lunch," said KC, ripping into a Swiss Roll package. "Mr. Español-Is-My-Life-and-I-Never-Got-Any-in-High-School got his tighty-whities in a bunch when I mouthed off to him. So, I got stuck at lunch writing, in Spanish, some crap about maturity. Do you think food deprivation is grounds for a lawsuit? Your mom does the law gig."

"Um . . ." said Fat Angie, her eyes on the Swiss Roll. "Yeah, but she's more into mergers and contract stuff."

"You want one?" said KC, holding up the Swiss Roll package.

"No. My mom's . . . she's kinda on me, you know." Fat

Angie covered her belly with her arms. "She says I'm not . . . um . . . that I . . ."

"What?" said KC.

"That I'm fat," she said, ashamed.

KC nodded, all the while pensively chewing. "What do you think?"

"Huh?"

"Well, do you think you're . . . overweight?" KC asked.

"Sure," said Fat Angie. "I mean, everyone does."

"You know, back in Beverly Hills, people thought I was *so* pretty . . ."

"'Cause you are," said Fat Angie, immediately feeling self-conscious. "Um . . . you know. Like in the way new girls from somewhere else who are total packages are. Um . . . that's not . . . um . . . what I . . ."

KC grinned. "Thanks."

Dramatic pause.

"But see, it's like, people are dense. Like, look at this package." KC held up the Swiss Roll wrapper. "Doesn't this Little Debbie chick look wholesome and happy?"

Fat Angie shrugged. "Yeah."

"If she ate this shit all the time, she'd be all diabetic and miserable. She's just a face. It's make-believe. It doesn't mean anything. You know?"

Fat Angie clearly did not know. More so, she did not know how to begin to know the complexities of KC's analysis of body image.

"Esther is always on about marketing being the devil," said KC. "And maybe I mostly see her POV but don't tell her."

Fat Angie nodded. She was good at nodding.

"There's just more to *you* than how you look," KC said, biting into the second Swiss Roll. "It's more than a package."

Fat Angie tugged once again on her jeans. They were camel-toeing again.

"But packages. I mean, if they're not all diabetes inducing," said Fat Angie, "they're kinda still important. Like . . ."

KC listened. Fat Angie struggled with such focused attention.

"Is it because no one treats you weird that you're not afraid to be who you are?" Fat Angie asked.

"I don't know," said KC. "I mean, I just moved here, so the level of weird is still relative to the level of mystery. Things weren't as easy back in the Hills."

"But you just said people thought you were pretty."

"They did," said KC, outlining an invisible heart with the toe of her boot. "Why are you the way you are?"

"Kinda by default," said Fat Angie. "And a host of mood-stabilizing drugs. Besides. Everyone thinks I'm crazy."

"OK, prescription drugs aside. What do *you* think?" KC asked.

The moment was clear. There. Vulnerability. Trust. Fat Angie had discussed the topic with her therapist to some length.

"I don't think people wanna see me," Fat Angie had said. *"I don't think they understand me."*

The therapist had made a note: *Potential borderline personality disorder with inability to take risks.*

"I don't know what I think," said Fat Angie. "I guess I think that I'm —"

Wang slammed into Fat Angie and knocked her off balance.

"Oops," said Wang.

He sized up the sultry KC.

"Yo, hey." Wang bit into an apple.

"Hey," said KC.

"This is Wang," said Angie. "My adopted brother."

"So . . ." Wang said, grinning ear to big ear. "You're the new girl."

"It's obvious, huh?" KC asked. "Well, I guess blending in wasn't really an option."

A horn honked. A woman waved at KC from a Toyota 4x4.

"Esther's here. I gotta split. Nice to meet you, Angie's brother," KC said, tugging Fat Angie away from Wang. "You wanna hang tomorrow? Esther's gonna be at the tattoo studio most of the day. We'd have the casa all to ourselves. I've got a stellar collection of indie rock on vinyl. It is absolute ultra."

"Yeah?" said Fat Angie.

"Coolness?" said KC. "What time —"

"No . . . um . . ." said Fat Angie. "I can't. I mean, I want to . . . but I have to go to this baby . . . shower thing party with my mom. It's a required family appearance."

"Sweet, I'm in," said KC.

"You wanna come to a baby shower party thing with me?"

"Oh, yeah. They always have the weirdest food. And the games. Have you ever played those jacked-out games?" said KC.

Fat Angie shook her head.

"Well, Esther's got four very fertile sisters. So baby showers are like Super Bowl parties. Absurd-weird fun."

"OK," Fat Angie said.

"Sweet, we're there," said KC. "Call me."

The buses lined up as KC slid into the truck. She flashed her right hand with pinky and thumb extended in "call me" mode.

"Hey," said Wang.

"I gotta get on the bus," Fat Angie said. "Since you never give me a ride."

"Anyway. What's the KC story?" said Wang.

"Like I would tell you?"

He shook his head. "Tell me or I'll stuff your toothpaste with Monistat again."

"She's new," said Fat Angie flatly.

"Duh. But what's her deal? Why is she so interested in you?"

"Because I'm a nice person," Fat Angie said. "You used to remember that before you went jerkface to me at school."

"Whatev . . ." He laughed. "Just remember, yo. No amount of new-girl cool is gonna make anyone forget your pep rally slash and thrash."

"F you," she said.

"*Oooo.* Another failed attempt at foul language. You're such a *fucking* saint," Wang said. "Fucking crazy saint just like—"

And before Wang could say their sister's name, Fat Angie shoved him. Hard! So hard that he fell flat on his butt.

Fat Angie was aware of the unwanted audience.

She started counting in her head.

The bus driver called out to her.

Wang stood, straightening out the handprints she had left on his shirt. "You're switch is flipped, and I'm telling Mom."

"Wang, c'mon. I'm sorry—I didn't meant to . . ."

"Get off me," he said.

The bus driver closed the doors. Fat Angie froze in place as Wang walked to his Jeep Cherokee.

"She'll never come back," he said. "Never!"

His voice was swallowed between chatter and bus-engine hum. Fat Angie beat on the bus doors with her palm four times, and it opened. Still counting in her head, she plopped into her usual seat. The Duo of Geekdom continued their spitball target practice. She leaned her head against the seat. Maybe Wang was right. Maybe she did not know how to "belong" in the absence of her sister. That was exactly what she had thought the day she'd slit her wrist with a discount double-edged razor. The main chorus of "Free Fallin' "—the Tom Petty song her mother had played on repeat for days after the disappearance was first announced—had echoed in Fat Angie's head as they lifted her into the ambulance.

She had told her therapist, *"I just couldn't get the song outta my head. It was exactly how I felt."*

The therapist had made a note: *Music therapy not an option.*

The bus was several stops in when Fat Angie realized she had never read KC's note.

Each unfold of the note revealed a graffiti-esque layer of hearts on one side. On the other, written in red ink, was

I think you rock too.
KC Romance

Fat Angie entertained the possibility that perhaps she could be the daredevil, the girl against the grain she had hoped to be. Because she was most definitely seen by one new-cool-swell girl, KC Romance!

Chapter SIX

Fat Angie stood over the full sheet cake. She had been standing there for three minutes according to the precision timing of her Casio calculator watch. The watch had been her father's when he was her age. Standing well within earshot, the Triple Threat spoke in cupped hand whispers. Fat Angie could feel their perfectly blue eyes boring a hole into the back of her skull. Their barrage of bubble-gum commentary shaped into a white noise balloon, encasing Fat Angie and the image of that cake. Then, *pop!* The piercing laughter of her mother burst the otherwise hypnotic moment.

"Oh, Debbie, that's the best story," said her mother in the voice she used only for social gatherings and Wang's therapist. The voice made Fat Angie's skin want to rip from the bone. She didn't quite know why.

Her mother picked up a dessert plate and a pink plastic knife and fork.

"What are you doing?" said Fat Angie's couldn't-be-bothered mother. "People have been staring at you standing here. You promised to reel it in."

"I can't eat that," Fat Angie said, her eyes still fixated on the cake.

"I said it was fine," said Fat Angie's mother. "You just have to skip dinner. Trust me, you will survive without one meal."

"It's a *fetus,*" Fat Angie said, looking at her mother.

The cake had an ultrasound picture on it. Fat Angie stared at its oddly shaped parts once again.

"It's an ultrasound of a baby," said her mother, annoyed. "And your aunt is very proud of it, so quit being so strange. People will never love you if you keep being so strange. Isn't that what your therapist told you?"

"Not in so many words," Fat Angie said.

"I see your eccentric new friend is enjoying herself," said Fat Angie's mother.

KC double dipped celery from the veggie platter while playing a baby-name game.

"Where did you say she was from?" asked her mother, sampling a cookie.

"I didn't," said Fat Angie, her eyes fixed on the motionless baby legs. "That really doesn't bother you? Baby legs waiting to be devoured?"

"It's a cake," said her mother. "I know you loathe my

side of the family. But sometimes you have to do things you don't want to do."

"Why are you talking to me like I'm five?"

"To be honest, I don't know how else to talk to you," said her mother. "You wanted to know."

KC plowed in, hanging over Fat Angie's shoulder. She smelled of Cherry Coke and vanilla-scented candles. "Game's over. They're doing karaoke in fifteen. I already put us in to sing . . ." KC tilted her head at the cake. "Is that a . . . ?"

"A fetus?" Fat Angie finished.

"It's not a fetus," her mother said in a mother-hush voice.

"WOW!" KC reached for her cell phone. "A fetus — on a cake!" She framed the picture with precision.

Fat Angie's couldn't-be-bothered mother reeked of incredibly bothered. She stared at KC and sized her up, just as she had when they'd picked her up. KC's fitted long-sleeved T-shirt with a feminist fist of empowerment on the front and WOMAN POWER stamped in red on the back had forced the room of pastels and pearls into fake hellos and queries of "Where did you get that lovely shirt?" (The one exception was a distant relative who harvested cage-free eggs. She absolutely loved the shirt.)

"Look," KC said, holding her cell screen to Angie. "Tell me that is not going to go viral."

Fat Angie's mother leaned into Fat Angie and whispered, "What is she doing?"

"Being normal," said Fat Angie.

Her mother cleared her throat and switched back to party voice. "KC, why did you say you moved here?"

"I didn't," said KC. "Say why. Guess there's no real super reason. Esther knew a guy in L.A. whose son bought in to a shop out here and they were looking for artists."

"Esther?" asked Fat Angie's mother.

Fat Angie began to sweat.

"My mom," said KC. "She works at Raise the Ink Tattoos on Hamilton. Across from Four Feathers Chicken and Daddy Low Records. She's wicked great." KC leaned in to Fat Angie's mother and pointed to her neck. "I had to *beg* her to do this though."

"That's a real tattoo?" said Fat Angie's mother, her voice losing its magic fakeness.

"M-hmm," said KC. "It was a massive pain. Literally. But it was like it was always there. The needle just sort of revealed it."

"That's *so* cool," said Fat Angie, a super massive grin in full spinout.

Connie, Fat Angie's mother, shifted her weight from her right foot to her left. Fat Angie noticed this gesture because it was the stance Connie took when preparing to berate or belittle something or someone.

"Well, not everyone has to come from a traditional family," said Connie.

Fat Angie witnessed the gears readying in her couldn't-be-bothered mother's eyes. Connie's lips parted when —

"Actually, we're pretty snore-traditional," said KC. "Jiffy Pop popcorn and Turner Classic Movies on Friday nights and family dinner *every* night. Esther thinks family dinner is important to my emotional growth or something Dr. Phil like."

"She's not really home for dinner much," blurted out Fat Angie about her mother. She had no conscious awareness of how absolutely out of order she had been until her mother hooked on to her arm and reeled her in for an ear chat.

"I told you not to talk about our personal lives," said Fat Angie's mother.

"What's personal about you never being home?" said Fat Angie.

"Connie," said a party guest, leaning in to Fat Angie's mother. "Everything OK?"

"Absolutely. Mother-daughter whispers," said Fat Angie's mother.

"Emily and I are the same way," said the woman, clearly a little tipsy on the shower sangria. "When I can get the iBud thingies out of her ears."

"Everyone over here," announced Fat Angie's bursting-pregnant aunt, Meghan.

Connie nudged Angie toward the table.

"Angie, what do you think about the cake?" asked Aunt Meghan.

Fat Angie's mother's eyes cut to her. Her pretend smile clearly conveyed that Fat Angie was not to say what she thought. The Triple Threat descended on the table, along with other guests.

"It's a fetus?" Fat Angie said.

"I know!" said her aunt. "It's absolutely amazing, isn't it?"

"Connie." Meghan held out the cake cutter. "As godmother of this new baby boy, will you cut the cake?"

Connie's face stretched to new lengths of fake smile. So much so that her right cheek shook ever so slightly.

And so Fat Angie's mother cut into the cake, dismembering the feet. Fat Angie flinched. Arms and legs . . . torso and toes. Fat Angie and KC backed away from the food table as women lined up, barbaric, cutting piece after piece, smiling and laughing, their mouths chewing on fetus image.

"Give me your plate," said Angie's mother.

Fat Angie reluctantly held her plate up. Part of a leg and foot stared back at her.

"Come sign up for karaoke," Meghan said to Connie. "We'll do a duet."

"Be right there," said Fat Angie's mother. Then, to Fat Angie, she said, "Eat the cake. Pretend to be interested in what someone else needs."

Fat Angie stood there as her mother reentered the posh-posh gathering of matching plates and cups. Why could Angie not simply play along? Be as her mother suggested — normal.

"Your mom's kinda different," said KC.

"I'm sorry," said Fat Angie.

"For?"

"I should've . . ." Fat Angie shook her head. "My family's a little complicated."

"That's not your fault," said KC. "Come to one of my so-called family reunions. A competition of Coach purses, fake-and-bake tans, and motorcycle hippies."

KC eyed Fat Angie's serving of cake. "Can I yum?"

Fat Angie passed the plate to KC, who picked up a fork and ate what Fat Angie imagined was a toe.

"It's fine," KC said, smiling with a smudge of gray icing on her upper lip. "Just eat it with your eyes closed. I do it with squid."

Fat Angie closed her eyes and ate very quickly — so quickly that her acid reflux refluxed. She sprinted out of the room.

Four and a half minutes later, clocked by her Casio calculator watch, Fat Angie was still on the bathroom floor. She had hurled only for the first minute and twelve seconds after jamming her finger down her throat like Marcy Winters on the cheerleading squad. She spent the rest of the time hunched on her knees, staring at the cake remnants floating in the toilet bowl. They did not resemble a person's image anymore. She could not understand why.

The 1970s hit "Ring My Bell" boomed from the living room. The drunken women sang off-key. Fat Angie began counting out loud as her therapist would have suggested. She began to digress.

The ambulance ride to the hospital . . . sirens wailing . . .

Fat Angie squinted. She drew her knees to her chest and counted aloud from one. The song seeped through. . . .

Her sister dribbling the basketball . . . crowds cheering . . . bombs . . . war . . .

"Lester hates his name. He won't respond to it."

She began counting from one again.

Children screaming on the CBS Evening News. There was blood — everywhere.

She counted louder, squinted harder. *Her sister—*

Fat Angie stopped.

She could not remember her sister's voice.

Pause.

Stop pause.

"One two three four five six seven . . ."

She counted so loud and ran the numbers together so quickly that she did not recognize the knocking on the door until —

"It's KC. You cool?"

"Um . . . just a second," said Fat Angie.

Fat Angie lowered the seat and opened the door.

"Hey," said KC. "Can I . . ." She motioned to come in.

Fat Angie perched on the toilet as KC leaned against the wall. Neither one of them really looked at each other for six and a half seconds.

"I hate parties like this," Fat Angie said. "These family things my mom drags me and Wang to. Well, when he's not incarcerated or off his Ritalin. She keeps trying to dress me in something with flowers and lace. Tells me how to walk and talk. And she does this laugh. Where it's, like, coming through her nose."

KC grinned. "Yeah, I kinda noticed."

"It's just really pathetic, you know?" said Fat Angie.

"Just because your family sucks doesn't mean you have to," said KC. "Not that I'm all Buddha-wise on some mountaintop. I just think everyone should carry their own baggage. Like at the bus station."

"Yeah," said Fat Angie.

"Look, let's bail. Go over to my place."

Fat Angie sighed, washing her mouth out at the sink. "My mom will spit branding tools if I leave."

"She'll get over it," said KC. "Not to mention she's on the distract. Some half-a-hunk showed up and they stepped out to his car."

"Sporty red with pleather seats?" asked Fat Angie.

"Yeah."

"I guess she's getting less worried about the PDA."

"Huh?" said KC.

"She's dating Wang's court-appointed therapist," said Fat Angie. She wiped her face with the underside of her frilly shirt.

"That's so weird," KC said, chuckling.

Fat Angie lowered her chin. It doubled.

"Look, if I sing you a song, can we bail?" asked KC.

"Seriously, I can't," said Fat Angie.

KC jumped up on the toilet, one foot on the tank. Her head was less than an inch from bumping the ceiling.

"KC," said Fat Angie.

KC sang.

"It's true there's nothing left to do
But let it all come right out"

"KC, please," Fat Angie said.

KC continued.

"The truth runs loose
And you really can't hide it now"

"C'mon, you know this one." KC grinned.

That beat thing occurred. Then, out of somewhere, Fat Angie's breath formed into a harmony.

Fat Angie softly sang with KC.

"No one else gets me
The way that you do somehow"

The girls grinned. KC continued, her voice full, alive . . .

"But everywhere you go someone's crying
And every turn you take you're scared of trying"

KC moved to the edge of the tub. She swung back and forth, gaining balance as she sang.

"But what if maybe
We could make it out crazy
We could make it out crazy
Past all these walls
We don't need at all"

KC smiled, for the first time seeming self-conscious. Fat Angie sobered up from her singing delirium.

"What?" KC said.

"My . . . my sister loves that song."

Fat Angie bit the inside of her cheek.

Pause.

More awkward pause.

They were swaddled in the uncomfortable pause.

KC stepped down from the tub edge. For such a large bathroom, the two girls were incredibly close.

"Hey," said KC.

"Hey," said Fat Angie.

"Um . . ." said KC. It was an unusual filler in her vernacular.

"Yeah?" said Fat Angie.

"So you wanna . . ." said KC.

"Yeah," said Fat Angie, unsure of what the "wanna" actually was.

Fat Angie's heart exercised at rapid heart pounding rate. Having KC so close—so deliciously vanilla-and-Coke–smelling close—automatically parted Fat Angie's closed lips. She could not explain the sensation swelling in her growling stomach. She was hungry but it was more. Much, much more. And when some clarity for Fat Angie's parted lips seemed to be on the horizon, KC unlocked the bathroom door and twisted the knob open.

Fat Angie gulped. Her parted lips smashed shut.

"C'mon," KC said.

"Um, yeah, OK," said Fat Angie.

KC slipped around her.

Fat Angie flushed the toilet and caught a glimpse of herself in the ornate mirror. A glimpse that became a stare. She tried to see the Angie beneath the fat. She tried to see her wrists without the scars. She tried to see a girl who could be brave like the woman in KC's song. But she just saw fat . . . Fat Angie.

Chapter SEVEN

Fat Angie stood behind KC, who was peering through her hands as though she were a director framing a shot.

"Sweet," KC said.

KC stepped back, critically admiring her newest installment, a five-by-seven copy of the cell phone pic of the ultrasound cake. It was plastered in with precision among a wall collage of Johnny Depp's tattoos, off-kilter postcards, artsy magazine clippings, and a 1950s ad encouraging women to eat tapeworms to stay thin. From the grin on her face, it was clear that her Wall of Thoughts So Twisted had reached masterpiece status.

"What do you think?" KC said.

Fat Angie was more uncomfortable with the image than she had been at the baby shower. The photograph was grainier than it had been on the cake, the result of a low pixel count on KC's camera phone. The picture reminded

Fat Angie of the printouts she had collected of the war in Iraq. Of the Shock and Awe bombings. Of terrains she had Google Earthed and circled in red marker as potential hostage havens for her sister.

"It's OK," said Fat Angie, sitting on the end of the bed.

But it wasn't OK.

"It's actually very disturbing," said KC, getting online to post the image on her various social networks. "I like that. People should be disturbed sometimes."

This was a peculiar notion to Fat Angie.

A sort of secret code knock thumped on KC's door.

"Yeah," said KC.

A woman in trendy rimmed glasses, which clashed with the faded vine tattoo twisting along her arm, poked her head in.

"Sorry, didn't know you had company," she said.

"Esther, Angie. Angie, Esther." KC hooked her arm across Esther's shoulder. "This is my hippie mama."

"Quit it," Esther said. "Good to meet you, Angie. The resident smart-ass has said a lot about you."

Esther shook hands with Fat Angie, who stared at the arm inked with fall leaves.

"Did you do that?" Fat Angie asked.

"The ink? Hell no, darlin'," said Esther. "My first ex—"

"Not my dad," KC interrupted.

"Don't get me going on your dad," Esther said to KC.

"Esther," said KC, struggling to remove her boots.

Esther grabbed the heel of KC's boot. With a few calculated pulls, the boot released.

"You know I hate these boots," said Esther.

"You hate that *Dad* bought me these boots. The boots themselves are fine," said KC.

"Yeah, yeah. You know, you coulda told me you'd be hanging around. I would've left you something in the fridge."

KC and Esther stood face-to-face.

KC said, "And what would that something be?"

Esther pinched KC's cheek. "A piece of your pretty face."

"Ha-ha," said KC. "Don't quit your day job."

Esther's attention fell to KC's forearm. The forearm that she was scratching beneath her T-shirt. Before Esther could reach for her arm, KC slid her hands in her back pockets.

"How was the baby shower?" Esther asked KC.

"Completely on the nine. I would've given it a ten but they didn't have caviar. Oh, they loved the shirt, by the way," said KC.

"I bet," said Esther.

KC dragged Esther to the Wall of Thoughts So Twisted. "Check this."

"Is that a . . . ?" said Esther.

"A fetus," said Fat Angie.

"Wow!" Esther said.

"Yeah," said KC. "Can you believe? Ultrasound pic on the cake?"

"Huh?" Esther said, tilting her head as if a new angle would give some different meaning to the image.

KC aimed her camera phone at Esther and snapped a picture.

"That better not end up on your Wall of Twisted," Esther said.

"We'll see." KC smirked.

"Angie, you need anything?" Esther asked. "I could bake some *taquitos.*"

Fat Angie shook her head, mostly because Mexican food gave her gas.

"Hey, paparazzo," Esther said to KC, who was framing up another picture. "I'll be in the basement with Mike."

"What's Mike doing here?" said KC.

"He wanted to get some practice in on that pig ear you scratched on."

"Don't knock my skills, Esther. Besides, that ear is old."

"I'll see ya'll later," said Esther. "Nice to meet you, Angie. Don't let her cynicism rub off on you."

No sooner did KC's door shut than Fat Angie said, "Pig's ear?"

"It's a tattoo practice thing," KC said, sliding backward in a desk chair and landing in front of her computer. "It's not alive or anything."

Regardless of the pig's status, a horrible pang welled up in Fat Angie. *Charlotte's Web* had been a childhood favorite.

However, she strongly objected to the death of Charlotte. While able to process the logic of Charlotte's death for heightened dramatic tension, twist in plot, she felt it was unnecessary.

"You cool?" said KC, clicking on the computer keyboard. "Esther can be a shock rock."

"Remember my mother?" said Fat Angie.

"Right . . ." said KC.

Wandering around the room, Fat Angie took note of a massive stack of vinyl records and boxes of unpacked clothes. Peeking beneath a Pink Floyd tee, Fat Angie saw half of a framed photo of KC. She bit the inside of her lip as she moved the shirt only a few centimeters to reveal KC cheek to cheek with a rather attractive pom-pom teen.

"Who's this?" said Fat Angie, holding up the frame.

"Nobody," said KC. "Just a girl I knew in the Hills."

Fat Angie studied the image and the shift in KC's posture at the computer. It was not a nobody. She was very pretty. A very, very perfect kind of pretty.

KC's phone beeped. She read the text and then tossed her phone in a basket of dirty clothes.

"Everything OK?" Fat Angie asked.

"Yeah. Just my dad. He's what I call a Sometimes Dad. He's only around some of the time and only when it gels for him."

"I like the boots he got you," Fat Angie said.

KC cracked a grin. "Yeah, he really didn't get 'em. That's just what I told Esther. He gave me plastic and dropped me at some megamall in Minneapolis. Said, 'Get whatever you like, sweetheart.' I kinda wanted to scream because he'd promised to go with me. So I bought a pair of six-hundred-dollar boots instead."

"Wow . . ."

"It was stupid petty," KC said, scratching at her shirt-sleeve. "I mean, he loves me. He's just really hard to talk to."

"Yeah . . ."

"Yeah?" KC asked.

"Yeah."

Beat.

KC peeled a postcard off the Wall of Thoughts So Twisted. She handed it to Angie. Dusk. A guy in a dusty white T-shirt stood in the middle of a road. Canyons filled out the space around him. A teardrop trailer accented with Christmas lights and a woman in the doorway. She had a pie in hand. Angie could not assign meaning to all the elements in the image, other than to call it artsy.

"You ever wish you could meet someone in a photograph?" said KC. "Like, ask that guy there what he was really thinking when the picture went *snap*?"

"Sure. I mean, I guess so. But it's . . . what you're saying . . . it's just make-believe."

Fat Angie plopped on the bed. Fidgeting with loose threads, she made a hole in the knee of her jeans.

"I'm supposed to stay in reality. Be grounded," Fat Angie said.

"Your shrink or your mother?"

Fat Angie shrugged. "Both, I guess. See . . ."

A hum spun inside of Fat Angie. Swirled with the taste of vulnerable and uncertain. Her lips parted for nothing but air.

"What?" KC asked.

"My sister . . . she signed up for the air force and was deployed to Iraq two years ago. She's been missing since February, which is nine months, seven days, and"—she eyed her Casio calculator watch—"eight hours. But she's not dead."

"I knew. About your sister," KC said. "I friended the Facebook page your father put up when she went missing. Plus . . . I saw you on *Dateline.*"

"You saw me on *Dateline*?"

"The two-part Valentine's Day special," said KC, turning to Fat Angie. "It was the one with you and your mom. Wang glassy-eyed stoned. Your dad via satellite from Seattle."

"You saw me on *Dateline*?"

"It seemed really hard. That cutaway money shot, the video clip. You and your sister. Playing basketball in the driveway against your dad and Wang. It was kinda Norman Rockwell. Well, a suburban and extremely diverse Rockwell."

"I am critically stupid," said Angie.

"No," KC assured Fat Angie.

"For some reason I just thought you didn't know. Which is totally stupid 'cause the whole world knows," said Fat Angie. "You could've said."

"What?" asked KC. "'What's it like to have your sister taken hostage?' Seems kind of a killjoy intro."

Fat Angie nodded, biting the inside of her cheek.

"I really . . ." KC said. "I liked you before I knew you. Well, at least I thought I would. You seemed real. And uncomfortable. You were the only one in that interview who was uncomfortable. That was comforting. So, when Esther said we were moving to Dryfalls, Ohio—which I was not jumping on the joy for—I don't know. I hoped we could be friends or something."

"You don't know me," said Fat Angie, rubbing the scars on her wrist.

KC rolled her chair across the room.

"OK. You like Where Did You Come From? Italian cream soda with two shots of vanilla. You support the fight against cancer." KC held up her yellow bracelet. "You care about your brother even though he's crazy mean in public. And you try to please your mother but don't know where to start. And you'd probably do anything to see your sister again."

"Anybody could know that stuff," said Fat Angie.

"Could they know I like you?" said KC.

Butterflies flapped their butterfly wings in belly time.

"Not that I'm not transparent," said KC. "Clearly, Jake knows."

Fat Angie, her stomach hatching cocoon after cocoon of butterflies, was unsure how KC was transparent. And what did Jake have to do with any of it?

"Jake knows what?" said Fat Angie.

"That I'm gay," said KC, as though it were obvious.

"Like, gay-girl gay?" said Fat Angie.

"Well, definitely not like funny-ha-ha gay," said KC. "Though I *am* a lot on the funny. It's the cynicism, Esther says."

"Does Esther know you're gay-girl gay?"

"You're totally weirding here," said KC. "I'm sorry. I thought . . . I thought you . . ."

"That I was gay-girl gay," said Fat Angie.

First the unexpected conversation with Jake at The Backstory about KC being different. Now. Now Fat Angie had been perceived as full-on gay-girl gay. But there had been no pamphlets. There had been no rainbow-in-the-sky epiphany. There had been nothing. Had there?

"Angie?" said KC.

There had been no dancing Care Bears blasting belly rainbows in Fat Angie's dreams either. But were Care Bears a symbol of gay-girl gay? She really had not been confident when discussing masturbation with her therapist. She did not know if she preferred Lady Gaga to the long-tongued

KISS singer Gene Simmons. But she did prefer either one of them to the image of Barbies when forced to choose. The Barbies were too perfect. Fat Angie did not like too perfect. That much she was certain of.

In truth, Fat Angie had not contemplated the notion of lip-to-lip contact with *anyone* as a serious possibility. That was until KC had been so close to her an hour earlier. In the bathroom. At the baby shower. Until then, the idea of anyone kissing her had been outside the realm of statistical reality. But there. With a collage of Johnny Depp's tattoos . . . with a framed photo of KC with a very, very perfect kind of pretty girl and a grainy printout of an ultrasound image on a baby-shower cake . . . Fat Angie was engulfed in a huge conundrum.

Pause.

Pause.

Look-down-at-your-shoes kind of pause.

"Look, I'm sorry," said KC, kick-rolling her chair back to the computer. "Let's just forget the reveal part of the conversation."

That was, as far as Fat Angie was concerned, impossible.

Could Fat Angie be releasing some gay-girl-gay vibe unknowingly? Clearly, being introverted was not the code key for the lesbian lockbox. Ellen DeGeneres was not introverted and was in all regards *very* gay.

"There it is," said KC.

Fat Angie stood behind KC.

"Now 4,059 Facebook junkies know that photos of embryos on baby-shower cakes are the new *it,*" said KC.

"That's a lot of friends," said Fat Angie.

"Most of those people don't know me," said KC. "It's like my dad says, 'It's not worth wasting your time letting people in.' But a cynic can still dream."

KC stood up. She was very, very close to Fat Angie.

Fat Angie's armpits began to sweat. "I think I'm gay-girl gay with you," she said.

"We're crystal, don't worry about it," KC said. "You don't have to say something because I blended the lines for a sec. We can just be friends."

Friends? Fat Angie marveled at how "be friends" dug into her chest like some Syfy channel heart-devouring creature. It . . . really hurt. She shifted her weight from one foot to the next and looked down.

"Cool?" KC said, leaning in to Fat Angie's eye line.

"Yeah," said Fat Angie. "The best kind. Right?"

KC grinned halfheartedly. "Sure," she said, and went back to the computer.

Fat Angie sat on the bed.

Maybe Fat Angie really preferred neither Lady Gaga *nor* Gene Simmons. Maybe it was because they were not really options. Could KC Romance be what she really preferred?

Fat Angie walked down the sidewalk of Oaklawn Ends, her mind swarming with the notion of potentially being gay-girl gay. The thought was both confining and freeing. But as soon as KC had revealed her liking for her, she had retracted it. Fat Angie was confused by this limited-time offer.

She was challenged to count beyond ten in her head as she neared her house. Desperate to clear her head, she mumbled the numbers under her breath. She stepped over the cracks in the sidewalk, not because of obsessive-compulsive disorder but because it somehow felt like a game. A game she played, of course, alone.

"Hey," said Jake, throwing an orange tennis ball to Ryan.

She was perplexed by his instigation of chit-chat again.

"Hey," Fat Angie said.

Ryan returned the ball and Jake threw it in Fat Angie's direction.

Ryan bounded in full sprint after it and tried to halt the bounce with his paws.

Jake and Fat Angie met in the middle of the street.

"What's up?" he said.

"Nothing," said Fat Angie. "That's not true."

"So . . . ?" he said.

"This is really strange," she said, tugging at her jeans.

His eyes were forced downward with the awkwardness of her tugging.

"What?" he said, tossing the ball for Ryan in the circle of the cul-de-sac.

"We don't talk, Jake," said Fat Angie.

"Yeah," he said. "I know. I mean, why would we? You know?"

"So . . . ?" said Fat Angie.

Ryan returned with the ball and stood between them for a cue. Jake reached down, tugging the ball back and forth. "You're a little badass. *Rrrawr* . . ."

Jake tore the ball away and hurled it.

"Are you into me or something?" said Fat Angie.

"Wow. Wait. How?" asked Jake.

"Forget it." She started to walk off, and he grabbed her arm.

"Listen, Angie." Jake cleared his throat. "You know. I think it's cool you think I'm hot."

"I don't . . . ," Fat Angie said. "I mean, you are, I guess. But no."

"Then?"

"Then why?" said Fat Angie. "Why stick up for me with Gary? Why give KC a hard time? She's, like, the only one in the whole school who gives me a fair break, Jake. And it's a pretty big school."

"I just—what do you know about her? You met her only a few days ago."

"I met you a few days ago," said Fat Angie, walking away. "And we have lived across the street from each other for years."

"It's not like your sister and I never played ball."

"Yeah, you and her. Sometimes *with* me, but not you and me," Fat Angie said, crossing her arms over her chest.

"Look, KC's not—I just think she's—"

"Gay?" Fat Angie finished.

"Yeah," said Jake. "For starters. And while smokin' hot, she's down with the ladies."

"So what?"

"Seriously?" Jake asked. "When people figure it out, they—"

"It's just gay."

"Drew Haligner. Cool guy. Cool grades. Cool at sports. Comes out. Boom! It's like a bomb nobody wants to get near."

"She's different. People won't care like they did with Drew."

"Even if that's true, she's got history," Jake said.

"History? What does that mean, and why does it even matter to you?"

"Maybe I just . . . care," Jake said.

"You? Everyone's rock star cares about Fat Angie?"

"Don't call yourself that," he said.

"Why? It's what everyone else does."

"Look, I dunno. I care. OK?"

"Right. That's like admitting to seeing the latest *Rocky* sequel. It doesn't happen. I'm not stupid, Jake."

"I don't think . . ."—he stretched his neck—"that you're stupid."

She raised an eyebrow. An unattractive gesture, as it made her lip simultaneously rise. She stopped the action.

Jake continued. "Before I moved here, I lost my uncle. I was . . . I don't know, six. But he was kinda my world. And then he just wasn't . . . there."

"And?"

Ryan returned with the tennis ball. "What happened with your sister . . . it makes sense that you came off the hinge. You two were tight. Playing basketball in the driveway . . . hanging out all the time. I could see how she always made sure you were OK. And now that she's—"

"She's fine," said Fat Angie.

Jake did not follow her absoluteness.

"You think she's *dead* but she's not," Fat Angie said. "That's what they're all trying to make me believe. Did my mom—did she get you to do this? Be all nice to me."

"No," said Jake. "It's just that . . . Angie, she's been missing for nine months."

"Missing," Fat Angie repeated. "That's *not* dead."

Jake took the ball from Ryan and pitched it into the backyard.

"Look," Jake said, "I'm just trying to help you out. And I guess I hurt your feelings. But I'm not gonna say sorry." He walked toward his house. "And don't ask me why."

Fat Angie had been about to ask why.

"Because I don't know why," said Jake. "Just doesn't seem right."

"And you're all . . . um . . . right. Right clothes, right family, right dog! You're oozing with right."

"No, I'm not," he said, turning back to her. "Your sister — she lit up this street, you know? But lights burn out."

"Did you steal that from the Morbid Hallmark Collection?"

"No, it's a Jake Fetch original."

Fat Angie stood there, minus the pseudoclever comeback.

"You're not the only one who lost something," Jake said. "This neighborhood — Dryfalls. We all lost."

"You don't know," said Fat Angie. "They *don't* know."

"Right," said Jake. "You've cornered the market on *know.*"

Awkward I-don't-know-what-to-do-now pause.

"You're weird," said Fat Angie. "You're weird and mean."

"People are mean to you," said Jake. "I know that. People are jerks — people are messed up in all kind of ways. People do . . . *stupid* stuff when they're freaked. And yeah, you freak them. But quit sizing me up with everyone else, like I'm some life-size cutout jockazoid. That really pisses me off, Angie."

He shook his head and spoke under his breath: "If only I knew what to do."

"About?" said Fat Angie.

"You wouldn't get it," he said.

Jake walked off to play fetch with Ryan in their perfectly manicured backyard. Edge to edge, Jake was the epitome of perfect. No matter what he said. He did not know the depths of her pain—her fight to keep her sister's memory alive. Regardless of the drugs the therapist pumped into her, they could not mute her love for her sister. They couldn't take away her hope.

And right then Fat Angie looked up. Not into the sun, because that would most likely have damaged her retina. It was the basketball hoop. She had unknowingly stopped underneath it. Day in and day out for nine months, there had not been a single sound of a basketball pound-swooshing through the net.

That was when it happened.

The idea came to her, the way ideas often did: out of nowhere. As if growing on an invisible tree above her head and suddenly ripe for the picking. Fat Angie knew what she had to do.

Try out for the William Anders High School girls' varsity basketball team.

Chapter EIGHT

During gym, the girls worked out in the state-of-the-art fitness room. Fat Angie breathlessly climbed on the elliptical. KC curled barbells with various weight lifting machines between her and Angie. Stacy Ann and her gym posse engaged in under-their-breath snide remarks as Fat Angie huffed and puffed her way through the workout. Her HORNETS' NEST T-shirt was drenched in sweat, pits to chest. Coach Laden took note of the girl's unusual effort on the elliptical. Laden blew her whistle and said, "Showers! Let's go."

Fat Angie had set a time limit and a climb tension and would not yet leave the elliptical. Follow-through had marked the golden path for her sister's unbelievable success on and off the court. Follow-through was the key to her sister's basketball shots and, as she had shared with Angie many times, was equally important to success in life.

"You just have to visualize," her sister had said, spinning the ball between her palms. *"Visualize, follow through, and let go."*

And like that, Angie had closed her eyes and shot the ball in perfect form. *Swoosh!*

"Don't ever be scared to let go," her sister had said, tossing Angie the ball.

Fat Angie had forgotten how much her sister wanted her to try out for the team. How much she'd wanted her to feel the high of charging down the court. Fat Angie had allowed her couldn't-be-bothered mother to fill in the hope with doubt—with ridicule. But if she were serious about attaining one of the two coveted spots on Coach Laden's championship varsity team, she would have to visualize and, most important, follow through.

"Angie," said Coach Laden. "Showers."

"Al . . . most . . . fin . . . ished," the panting girl said.

The machine finally beeped.

Fat Angie held on to the rails for shaking-arm dear life. This follow-through would be harder than she had estimated.

"You feeling all right?" said Coach Laden.

"Yeah," said Fat Angie. "I'm . . . just working . . . out."

"It's good to work out hard," said Coach Laden. "But don't push it."

Fat Angie wiped her face with the stained neckline of her HORNET'S NEST T-shirt as she shuffled toward the locker room.

"Angie," said Coach Laden, tugging at a basketball charm on her thin gold necklace. "Good hustle."

"Thanks," said Fat Angie.

Fat Angie dragged herself around the corner of the fitness room, where KC was waiting.

"Hey," said KC.

"Hey," said Fat Angie, her response jam-packed with awkward.

"Waved to you in there," said KC.

"Yeah. I saw you. Wave."

KC nodded as they walked toward the locker room. "Huh. Thought you might wave back. 'Cause that's kinda what friends do."

"I did," said Fat Angie. "Didn't I?"

"Nope," said KC.

"I meant to. I'm just really focused."

"Share?" asked KC.

"You'll think it's lame," said Fat Angie.

"Benefit of the doubt can go a long way. Hit me."

Fat Angie mapped out a series of sentences in her head. The details were precise and well written but got stuck in Fat Angie's brain traffic.

"Is this about the other day?" KC asked. "If my proclamation of interest in you other than a friend freaked you later, you just gotta say. I just . . . I don't know."

"No," said Fat Angie. "I'm not freaked. Really."

"OK. So, we're a ten?"

Fat Angie did not follow the question. This was marked by her dumbfounded expression.

"Sorry. Midwest translation. All good?"

"Sure. Yeah. Definite ten."

"Sweetness. So . . . I'll catch you?" said KC,

"Yeah, definitely caught — catched. Catch."

"Swell," KC said, disappearing into the locker room.

Fat Angie stood there, becoming increasingly cold in her damp clothes. She had wanted to make some other declaration. Butterflies for a girl named Romance and a hunger for basketball. The scramble of it all was like being taken to an all-you-can-eat buffet the day after gastric bypass surgery.

Fat Angie looked down the court. Beyond the hoop and backboard. There, on the wall, hung six banners. Five all-region and one state win. Her sister's win.

Her sister would know exactly what to do — the best course of action. She was capable of navigating the complicated. She was beautiful and strong. She did not have a sum total of six scars on her wrists. She had not tried to take her life. Her sister lived life and fought for everyone else's.

That made Fat Angie mad right then. Mad that she — that she could not . . .

Fat Angie began counting in her head. *Calm down.* She simply needed to calm down.

"Counting will make you calm," her therapist had said, early in their sessions. *"It's like eating."*

Fat Angie had thought it was in no way like eating. *"The caloric intake is grossly different,"* she'd said.

"Just count," he had said.

The therapist had made a note: *Ability to process is stunted. Discuss the possible need for special services with mother.*

Fat Angie swung the locker-room door open. A small pocket of girls laughed. Fat Angie had failed to notice that she had continued counting aloud from the door to her locker, over a distance of approximately seven feet and four inches.

Stacy Ann straddled the bench near Fat Angie. "You training for the whale Olympics?"

Fat Angie stopped counting.

"Yeah, Stacy Ann, that's what I'm doing," Fat Angie said, slipping a hoodie over her HORNET'S NEST T-shirt.

"No wonder you always stink," said Stacy Ann. "You never take that *buzzzz* shirt off. Even your brother thinks you're a pig and he's a tool times eleven."

A shaky breath escaped Fat Angie's lips. Stacy Ann cackled.

Ignore, ignore, ignore the mean crank-ho with the DADDY'S GIRL *heart charm on her necklace,* Fat Angie thought. She kicked off her sneakers and was midway into putting on her jeans when Stacy Ann hooked her from behind. She pulled on Fat Angie's pudgy arms and dragged her off the bench.

"Get off of me! Get off!" said Fat Angie, her jeans rolling to her knees.

Many of the girls cheered Stacy Ann on as she dragged Fat Angie into the showers.

"You're not stinking up fifth period," said Stacy Ann.

The shower beat down on the two girls. Fat Angie inhaled water and coughed, "Stop!"

Stacy Ann yanked the hoodie over Fat Angie's head. Fat Angie's socks, sopped in water, slid along the shower floor. Stacy Ann had Fat Angie's T-shirt nearly off when KC grabbed her and threw her against the shower wall.

"Why are you such a sadistic bitch?" KC said. "What has she ever done to you?"

Stacy Ann wiggled loose and slammed KC to the floor. Water splashed. The girls rolled around and not gracefully. There were no stunt doubles. There was no good humor in this fight. It was, as many would say, *on*.

Fat Angie watched as fists were thrown. Blocks were made. The girls who had gone quiet launched back into "FIGHT, FIGHT, FIGHT!" mode.

Neither Stacy Ann nor KC seemed to really be winning, though.

Coach Laden peeled through a series of shoulders. "What's going on here?"

The coach separated Stacy Ann and KC, but the two made a final attempt at continuing their brawl.

The gym girls stood around, unsure how to play their hands as spectators. Coach Laden saw Fat Angie still wedged in the corner of the shower, half-dressed, drenched, and trembling.

"Who started this?" said Coach Laden.

Stacy Ann shot a dart of a look to Fat Angie. *Narc and die.*

"Who started this?" repeated Coach Laden in a not-so-lovely tone.

"Fat Angie," said one girl.

"She was talking trash to Stacy Ann," said another.

"That's bullshit," said KC, turning off the spigot of water beating down on Angie.

"You OK there?" said Coach Laden, her eyes on KC's exposed arm.

KC looked to Fat Angie. KC was bleeding.

"Yeah," KC said, hiding her arm. "Three karat all the way."

"Everyone get dressed," said Coach Laden.

KC shook her head and got up in Coach Laden's grill. "That's it? That's all you're gonna do?"

"Get dressed," said Coach Laden.

Stacy Ann smirked at KC.

KC continued. "One, I already am. Two, Stacy Ann is a megabitch—"

"Screw you, KC," said Stacy Ann.

"Enough," Coach Laden said.

"You, of all people, should be fair," KC said, charging off.

"Stacy Ann," said Coach Laden.

"Yeah, Coach?" Stacy Ann asked.

"You ever pull anything like this again, I don't care how many people say you didn't do it. I don't care if your *mom* is head of the PTA and calls me twelve times a day. I'll have you suspended for the year. Clear?"

Stacy Ann gritted her teeth. "She's not so special."

"Am. I. Clear?" Coach Laden repeated.

Stacy Ann nodded.

Fat Angie watched the exchange. She knew that even the likes of one Coach Laden could not stop the hate machine that was Stacy Ann Sloan.

"And you've got detention for two weeks," said Coach Laden.

"What?" said Stacy Ann.

"Wanna make it three?"

Stacy Ann glared at Fat Angie. "Two is great, Coach."

"Now get changed."

Coach Laden kneeled beside Fat Angie, who drew her knees in and raised one shoulder while turning her head down. Water drip-dropped from the ends of her hair to her nose. Coach Laden reached for her but Fat Angie pulled back. Only there was nowhere to go.

"It's not going to happen again," said Coach Laden.

Fat Angie shook her head . . . a lot. She breathed short, shallow breaths.

"It's not going to," said Coach Laden.

The tears welled. Fat Angie shot her eyes left to right to

prevent any crying. This was not the time for revealing tears. Coach Laden would find her too weak. Too special. Special in the way that would not fit her goal of making the varsity team. Nevertheless, Fat Angie was frozen in place.

"Looks like the new bad girl has a good heart," said Coach Laden.

Fat Angie, her mind too occupied with inhibiting emotion, did not track the trajectory of Coach Laden's comment.

"KC stuck up for you," said Coach Laden. "That's pretty impressive when you're new."

"Because I'm a freak?" Fat Angie said.

"You're not a freak, Angie," said Coach Laden, repositioning her squat. Her black Adidas with yellow soles squeaked.

"If you call my mom, she's gonna be really mad," Fat Angie said.

"Then we don't call. You haven't done anything wrong. Have you?"

Fat Angie shook her head.

"Then we'll toss your clothes in the dryer," said Coach Laden. "Suit you up in some athletic gear."

"Like it'd fit," said Fat Angie.

"Hey," said Coach Laden. "You can fit."

Coach Laden helped Fat Angie up.

As the two walked out, three things came to Fat Angie's mind. Would her clothes shrink? Should she wish for telekinetic powers now that the girls had officially taunted and laughed at her in the locker room? Though they had not thrown tampons. Was that critical to Carrie's rage at the end of the film? *Stop,* she told herself.

Stop, she told herself again. *Stop, stop, stop.*

Stop it, fat ass!

That wasn't her voice. Wang's school persona had injected itself into the commentary.

Fat Angie inhaled.

Fat Angie exhaled.

Fat Angie returned to *Carrie* once more, and then the word *STOP* flashed in her head, the way it appeared at the bottom of standardized tests.

With the notion of her clothes potentially shrinking in the dryer, *Carrie* discarded, and Wang's voice muted, Fat Angie was led to her final thought. The longest thought. The one that held her steady without the need for counting numbers in her head or aloud.

Why had KC hidden her arm?

After school, Fat Angie sought out KC Romance. Concerned that she would miss her bus, Fat Angie set the timer on her Casio calculator watch, allotting enough time to do a Fat Angie–style sprint to the bus.

KC was not at her locker.

She was not in the bus line.

She was not by the vending machines, in the cafeteria, in the gymnasium, or at the giant Hornet statue in front of

William Anders High School. Then, at some distance, Fat Angie spotted the long-legged KC stepping down a sidewalk. Fat Angie eyed her watch. She accounted for the time to catch up with KC, to resolve any miscommunication, and to still make her bus. Through this flurry of mathematical calculations, Fat Angie concluded that she could not do it all. And simply catching up to KC without any discussion would surely not improve the strained situation. But avoiding her altogether and hoping to patch it over with a text message could also leave her on the losing end. Fat Angie remembered KC had referred to herself as "old-school" and preferred handwritten notes. There was no time for such a labor-intensive effort.

Fat Angie went into a Fat Angie overload.

Too much, too much, too much!

Why were there so many alternatives? So many different outcomes to be considered?

Fat Angie's watch beeped. She'd wasted too much time deliberating. It was, as the cliché went, now or never. Do or die. A girl against the grain — the metaphor seemed clear.

Fat Angie sprinted Fat Angie–style toward KC. Her backpack slapped against her back. The feeling was quite uncomfortable. In fact, it hurt like all hell. She tripped and fell arms-first onto the concrete with the grace of girls in horror films. The casualty: her right elbow.

It bled.

Fat Angie hated blood.

She once had told her therapist, *"It isn't at all like on TV. When you bleed, it really is something."*

The therapist had made a note: *Obsession with notions of self-mutilation.*

The injury on Fat Angie's elbow was minor. She wiped it on her jeans. It stung.

Fat Angie still had KC in her sights as the beauty turned a corner. She ran once again. Backpack back-slapping her. "KC," called Fat Angie.

Between the elliptical in gym and the run, Fat Angie was spent.

"Go away, Angie," said KC.

"Wait," said Fat Angie, catching up.

"You're gonna miss your bus," said KC.

"Already did," Fat Angie said, winded. "See, I set the timer to estimate—"

"Angie," said KC. "Stop."

Fat Angie was perplexed. And still trying to catch her breath.

"When we—you and me at The Backstory," said KC. "The way we talked. I just. I *wanted* things to be different here."

"It's Dryfalls," said Fat Angie. "Everything's different. We don't even have an IHOP."

"That's not what I mean."

"Um . . ." said Fat Angie. "I didn't think so. It sounded a lot funnier in my head. Like when I told my therapist he reminded me of James Dean in *Giant.* Well, a cartoon version. A fatter, hair-receding version with an overbite. Actually, he doesn't look like James Dean at all. Maybe that's why that wasn't so funny either."

KC laughed. Not a big bursting laugh. More of that quick-breath kind.

Fat Angie smiled, and the left side of her mouth inched just a bit higher into an adorable dimple.

"What are you doing, Angie?" KC tugged at her messenger bag strap.

"I don't know," said Fat Angie. "I mean, I do. But I don't."

"Look, I gotta split," said KC, heading down the sidewalk.

Fat Angie was in a classic Fat Angie scenario. The urge to purge the thoughts in her head were locked behind serious mood-controlling medications and her fear of rejection. She dropped her head back and stared at a breath of white clouds. Fall leaves falling, raining with a burst of wind. Spinning orange, yellow, and red . . . dancing. She felt the moment was poetic — metaphorical — no, poetic. At least pretty.

"KC," said Fat Angie.

Romance stopped for Fat Angie. "Yeah."

Fat Angie hustled over to KC. Convinced her move would be smooth and dramatic, she froze.

"Um . . ." said Fat Angie. "Thank you."

"For?"

"For?" Fat Angie said, a sense of panic in her voice.

The *for* was clear. Crystal. But Fat Angie stood there in the pretty, poetic-falling-leaves moment, saturated in her typical awkwardness.

"Um . . . for being the new girl who stood up for me," said Fat Angie, channeling Coach Laden. "And . . . what . . . what is *that*? I mean, why . . . did you hide? Your arm?"

Fat Angie eyed KC's arm.

"It's nothing, Angie."

"That doesn't make . . . that doesn't make sense. You have too many nothings," said Fat Angie. "The girl in the picture frame in your room. No one frames a nothing. Unless their grandmother gave it to them. And that was way not a grandmother-type picture."

"Just leave it," said KC.

"I care," said Fat Angie.

"You don't know me."

"So?" said Fat Angie. "It's only a technicality. People get married in Las Vegas all the time and they don't know each other. Not that I think we should—"

"I'm a cutter, OK?" said KC. "But on the record, the slice and dice is about me. And I don't even do it anymore. I mean, I had a slipup, obviously, but it was super micro."

"KC, I don't really know what that means," Fat Angie said.

KC stretched her neck and clung to her messenger bag

strap. "It means you shouldn't always judge the package. It's what's inside that really sucks sometimes. I dunno. It's hard to explain. It's just how I deal . . . *did* deal a lot in the past. But it's over."

KC, speaking in KC speak, had revealed a hint of her ouch, pain — vulnerability. As with many things about KC Romance, this reached right into the chest of Angie. Not Fat Angie but Angie. This perplexed her. Intensely.

The moment was ripe for some brilliant reply. The thought spun around and around Angie's fatty-acid mind: WWMSD (what would my sister do)?

Follow through. She would follow through.

Angie undid her Casio calculator watch and revealed three deep, erratic scars.

Beat.

KC's long fingers, nails finished with black polish, slid over the scars. To be seen — to be touched — Angie could not remember such a time since her sister had disappeared. After the scars — and the headlines and the camera footage of Angie's pep rally meltdown — her couldn't-be-bothered mother had moved into rare avoidance form. Not that she had ever been a very demonstrative person — not even with Angie's sister, and she had seemed to want it more than any of them. Well, maybe her dad wanted it too.

The fall leaves fell.

A car drove by.

A dog barked. Then again. Then again.

"All better," said KC, taking her hands away from Fat Angie's wrist.

And for a moment, it was.

"Can I see?" Angie asked, holding on to KC's wrist. "Under your sleeve?"

"It's not required. Ever. OK?" said KC.

Angie gulped, feeling more like Fat Angie all over. Holding KC's wrist, she said, "I still think you rock."

KC's eyes softened. "I think you rock, too."

The moment was combustible. Their eyes were in an I-can't-stop-looking-at-you-or-I'll-die lock. KC leaned forward, head tilting, lips parting, when—

"Fucking dykes!" blared from Gary Klein's mouth out the passenger window of an SUV. The driver laid into the horn.

Fat Angie's hand fell away.

KC adjusted her posture. Crossing her arms, she established an invisible wall as she shook her head at the bitter irony.

"It's always the same school," said KC. "Whether you have an IHOP or not."

Fat Angie was not accustomed to any of what had just almost transpired. She did not like to see KC so down on herself.

"I gotta fly," said KC. "Esther . . . pseudotraditional dinner in an hour."

"OK," Fat Angie said.

KC started to reach for Fat Angie's face but caught herself. "You really are beautiful."

And just like that, KC Romance walked away from Fat Angie.

This time, Fat Angie did not follow.

Chapter NINE

Fat Angie removed her sister's DVD/VCR combo player from the hall closet. The DVD player was broken but jammed into the VCR was *Magic Johnson Presents: Fundamentals of Basketball.* This would be her primary training tool because her sister had studied the video many a time before and during basketball season. Her sister held Magic Johnson (former Los Angeles Laker who contracted HIV in the 1990s) in the highest regard, so he would now be Angie's mentor for at least fifty-two minutes out of every hour until tryouts—factoring in time for school, hands-on practice drills in the driveway, and sleep.

Just as her sister had done her freshman year, Fat Angie would rise to the occasion. Against all odds, she would earn a coveted spot on the Hornets' Nest varsity basketball team. In spite of the technicality that it was, in fact, Fat Angie's repeat of freshman year. Such technicalities did not register with Fat Angie. Besides, there was too much work to be done.

The days passed and Fat Angie saw very little of KC outside of gym class. Fat Angie's heart swelled for the leggy girl toting her Last Supper lunch box to the cafeteria, where she always sat alone. The two occasionally exchanged looks through a sea of shoulders and bobbing heads. Angie's urge to say something to KC was complicated by her not knowing *what* to say. The paralysis of such a paradox kept the girls together yet apart.

Jake had become an avid onlooker of Fat Angie's after-school basketball drills. So had a few of her other neighbors in Oaklawn Ends. The neighbors were hoping to catch a glimpse of the wunderkind that had been Fat Angie's sister. What they saw instead was Fat Angie. Fat Angie in her sister's HORNETS' NEST T-shirt.

One afternoon, Jake watched from his living-room window as Fat Angie ran drills in her driveway. A crooked line of metal folding chairs and a baby stroller served in place of orange safety cones on the concrete slope for her to dribble between. Ball-handling drills were key according to her sister and Magic Johnson.

"You can't shoot if you can't control the ball," her sister had said on more than one occasion as they practiced in the driveway. *"But remember, the free throw will always save you."*

Often, Angie had been the "practice dummy," playing

the defender for her sister early in the morning and late at night. While Angie was not as fat then, she was nevertheless heavy. And while her weight had slowed her down, she, like her sister, had a keen sense of the game. In those days, Fat Angie played against lightning in motion. And sometimes she even scored. When that happened, Angie's sister goaded her to dream big. To stay focused. To never quit.

"Hey, Angie," called Jake, coming out of his house, Ryan clicking behind him.

"Now you're talking to me?" she said.

"I haven't not talked to you," he said, leaning on the back of his father's antique Mustang.

She straightened her back, a definite soreness just about everywhere in her body. "That makes no sense," she said.

"Yeah it does," he said.

"Does not."

"Yeah," he said.

"You're weird," she said. "You know that, right? How you try to . . . fit . . . everything."

"You're still on that?" said Jake. "Even if you know it pisses me off?"

"It's good to make people uncomfortable sometimes," Fat Angie said.

Fat Angie began the awkward experience of the jump shot. Jake and Ryan sat on their curb and watched her uncoordinated body attempting to coordinate.

Coordinate (v): to make moving parts, such as parts of the body, work together in sequence or in time with one another, or to work with another person in this way.

Jake chomped into an apple. He chomped again. And again. And again.

He patted Ryan on the head and said, "Let's go, boy," and they crossed the street to Fat Angie's driveway. The basketball ricocheted off the rim and bounce-rolled to Ryan's paw. The dog barked.

"What are you doing?" said Jake, snapping up the ball and sinking a free throw with nothing but net.

Fat Angie rebounded the ball.

"I'm going out for the varsity team," she said, peeling her sweaty hair from her forehead.

"You're joking, right?" he said.

"Do I seem funny?" she said.

"No. It's just . . ." Jake struggled how to state the obvious. "Varsity's competitive. I don't even play varsity, and I'm really good."

She glared.

"Not that you aren't," he said, backpedaling with great speed. "It's just not as easy as saying you're gonna go out for the varsity team."

"Why?" she asked.

Jake snapped the ball from her hands. He dribbled, spun, and went up in the air with a beautiful jumper.

"Just 'cause," he said.

She rebounded the ball. "I'll practice all night. Every night. Just the way I have been. See?"

She pointed to the side of the two-car garage. Three floodlights on yellow stands were clumped together.

"Yeah, I've seen you out here stumbling around," he said.

She moved into position for a jump shot and failed miserably once again.

Jake snapped up the rebound. "What's really going on? KC put you up to this?"

"No!" she said. "We don't even talk, OK? Give me the ball."

She held her hands out. Jake whipped the ball up and spun it on his index finger. This was not only an act of skill, but as Fat Angie thought, showing off.

"You really wanna go out for varsity?" he said.

"Yes." She made for the ball, but the nimble Jake, in full finger spin, jerked it from her.

"Because of your sister?" he asked.

"Because of me."

Fat Angie would not be dissuaded. And the only way the good-hearted Jake could think to protect her was to help her. Jake whip-spun the ball on his finger before holstering it in the crook of his arm.

"OK," he said. "But you gotta be serious."

"I am."

"Then you better know Coach Laden is a sucker for a solid jump shot and killer defense. I've seen her," said Jake.

"I've been to a game."

"Yeah, but now you wanna *play* in one," said Jake. "You'll have to show her you've got teeth."

Fat Angie stretched her lips, revealing that, in fact, she did have teeth. Jake looked down at Ryan. Ryan barked.

"Um . . . that was kinda funny," she said.

Jake half-laughed.

"Now, the jump shot is all about flow," said Jake, who began the visuals. "You dribble. Full stop. See? Bend your knees and fly straight up. Before you come down, release, and . . . full follow-through. See how I flicked my wrist? It puts a strong-ass spin on the ball. And you always have a target. Once you get the form it's all about what you see. And see only one thing: your target. Everything else is invisible."

Jake pushed a chest pass that knocked Fat Angie harder in the bosom than she would have anticipated.

Pause.

"What?" Jake said.

"I'm writing a letter to my sister," said Fat Angie. "I've been writing it since my mom locked me up in that rehab place." Fat Angie aggressively kicked the toe of her sneaker against the concrete driveway. It left a hint of a mark. "Everyone wants me to think she's dead, Jake. Even you."

Jake seemed unprepared for such dramatic statements.

Even if his life wasn't perfect, it was no way as screwed up as Fat Angie's. Jake's life consisted of:

mom + dad + dog = ☺

Fat Angie's life equation was

couldn't-be-bothered mom – dad – sister
+ misfit adopted brother = ☹

Fat Angie stood there, awkwardly tugging at her sister's HORNETS' NEST T-shirt, which was sticking to her. Jake looked at Ryan and said, "Then she's not."

Ryan wagged his tail.

"What about everything you said? Um, about how long she's been gone," said Fat Angie.

"Hey, I'm just a jock. Arrogance is sort of in the handbook."

"A freak jock," she said, chest-passing the ball back to him.

"Takes one to know one." He slammed the ball back to her.

"Wacko," she said, passing the ball.

"Crazy." He passed the ball back.

They continued the firing of back-and-forth ball passing until Fat Angie abruptly said, "I'm gay-girl gay with KC Romance."

Jake held on to the ball. "Really?" he said, a little too serious for her comfort.

She crossed her arms over her stomach.

"Yeah, I think," she said. "I think, maybe. Yeah. I don't know."

He dribbled away from the basket. "I knew she was, but I wasn't sure you were. She's got a history, you know."

"I know about the cutting thing," Fat Angie said.

Jake powered hard to the basket. Up. Flying. Slam dunk! The cutest little boy smile cut the edges of his mouth.

"She is really hot," he said, throwing the ball back at Fat Angie.

Angie, with what most would deem a dorky expression, smiled and basked in Jake's description. "Yeah. But it's different."

"Not really," said Jake, hands ready for the ball. "But yeah. It is."

"I think she could really like me . . . does like me. Uggh. What do I do?" She fired the ball back to him.

He ripped the ball right back at her. "I don't know. I mean, I'm not a gay-girl-gay guru. Just make sure you know what you're getting into. You know?"

Angie nodded.

"That's what your sister would say, right?" Jake said.

"Yeah," she agreed, noticing that Jake knew so specifically what her sister would have said. It was a strange thing for him to mention.

"Come on," he said. "Let's play."

Fat Angie practiced and practiced well into the evening

for several evenings with Jake. Her couldn't-be-bothered mother remained unbothered, as she was apparently working late every night. During this time of intense training, Wang watched his sister from his second-floor bedroom deck.

She ignored the increase in Wang's nasty remarks at school and the way he started to bring his school persona home. When he hinted at tearing her down, she would build herself back up by running basketball drills. Taking to the driveway every afternoon, Fat Angie had attracted an unexpected crowd. The neighbors of Oaklawn Ends began to act in a way that could only be characterized as peculiar. They mowed their lawns even though they had just been mowed. Some organized their garage though they were, by all accounts, already organized. The sound of a basketball beating the driveway had stopped with her sister. The resurgence of the game Jake and Fat Angie played intrigued them, and something about that felt right to her.

And so the neighbors went to bed to one sound: dribbling. And while Fat Angie practiced long past the designated noise-ordinance time, not a single neighbor called the police to file a complaint. They all wanted, in some way, to remember the wunderkind that had made Oaklawn Ends a beginning.

Chapter TEN

It was a Monday. It was cold and damp, and by all accounts the heat was on the fritz in the Hornets' Nest gymnasium. Fat Angie's fingers ached, but the soreness of her somewhat lighter body fell by the wayside. She stood, shoulders back, eyes steady on the huddles of girls waiting to try out for the varsity team. She stood alone, basking in the glory that her gym shorts were not as tight. Her biceps were chiseled into a shape that popped when she flexed. Her chin failed to double so easily when she looked forward. Fat Angie may not have had a body worth promoting according to any number of fashion magazines on the market, but it was a healthier, stronger, and, quite honestly, ready-to-kick-ass-and-take-names body.

With her sister's photo in the back pocket of her shorts, carefully sealed in the plastic photo protector of her Velcro wallet, Fat Angie was bigger and badder than ever. Nothing could keep her from making the team.

Well, almost nothing.

In expensive high-top sneakers and name-brand socks, Stacy Ann Sloan stepped on the court. Stacy Ann had played JV basketball the year before, her freshman year. She had been a thing to watch. It was only natural for her to gun for a spot on the varsity squad. Until that moment, Fat Angie had blocked out the natural order of such things.

Fat Angie's palms were damp and clammy, and they left a noticeable streak of wet on her hair as she brushed it away from her face.

Stacy Ann crossed the court toward Fat Angie, who nervously shifted her stance. It seemed to be the makings of a throw-down. In a battle of the good, the bad, and the fat, Stacy Ann seemed to have the upper hand. With beauty and athletic prowess in Stacy Ann's favor, Fat Angie would seem to have no chance of outshining the star of the William Anders JV basketball team in gunning for one of those two coveted varsity spots.

As Stacy Ann's eyes zeroed in on those of Fat Angie, she said, "Get off my court, Fatso."

Fat Angie's fingers fluttered at her side as if readying to reach for a weapon of mass destruction — the Swiss Roll squished in her shorts pocket. A weapon useless against the anorexic-in-training Stacy Ann, whose lips only touched romaine salads sprinkled with Craisins prepared by her Lexus-driving mother, a woman who most people thought was living well beyond her means. Though Fat Angie had never questioned why. Her mind was distracted by that for 4.7 seconds as she stared at the timer on her Casio calculator watch.

"What?" asked Stacy Ann.

Fat Angie was ripped back into reality by the shrillness of Stacy Ann's question. A girl whose sweet tooth was soothed only by four extra packets of Splenda on her Cheerios and two twenty-ounce Diet Cokes per day.

She was, by all standards of high-school girls, healthy.

Coach Laden, who had been otherwise occupied in the equipment room, stepped on the court and blew her silver whistle with flair. "Line it up against the wall," shouted Coach Laden. "Hustle!"

The group of hopefuls fell in, but Stacy Ann and Fat Angie continued their stare-down at the three-point line. Fat Angie knew that Coach Laden did not tolerate dissension in the ranks. She was the law. The long, long, very toned arm of the law. Basketball was her life, her imprint to leave on the world. Laminated and duct-taped to her office door, a sign read:

TEACHING
DRIBBLING, PASSING,
AND SCORING
ONE GIRL AT A TIME

Coach Laden tugged at the basketball charm she always wore. *A half of what is surely a whole basketball,* Fat Angie thought.

"Stacy Ann," called Coach Laden.

Stacy Ann clipped Fat Angie's shoulder as she joined the team. Fat Angie stood there, as awkward as a cow in a stadium full of butchers. It was her versus the Army of Stacy Ann. Fat Angie felt her knees nearly buckle.

"Angie," said Coach Laden. "What are you doing here?"

"I'm trying out," said Fat Angie.

Coach Laden put her arm around Fat Angie and led her off the court. "You know you're special," she said.

"Yes," confirmed Fat Angie.

Fat Angie kicked her eyes to the line of girls spectating from the edge of the basketball court.

"You see, Angie, basketball is a gutsy sport. It requires agility, quickness—"

"I've been practicing," Fat Angie said. "I *feel* I can play basketball."

"I want you to understand," Coach Laden said, "that you are *special.*"

The word *special* resonated somewhere deep in her. Deeper than she could have fully realized, until she said, "If you say that I'm *special* one more time, I'll scream."

Coach Laden, thrown off her well-meant play, lifted her arm off the Charmin-like shoulders of Fat Angie.

"I tried to kill myself," said Fat Angie. "So what—I

should sit in my room and be *special*? I'm tired of being *special,* Coach Laden. Just give me a chance."

"I don't want you to get hurt," said Coach Laden. "I don't want you . . . to be hurt anymore."

Fat Angie took a moment. A beat. That theater thing.

Then she walked past the well-sculpted coach and stood at the end of the line of girls. Laden was taken aback by Fat Angie's tenacity. This was evidenced by the coach's subtle grin.

Coach Laden stood center court. "We've got two spots and two spots only, so make these next two days count."

Fat Angie smiled to a girl beside her who, in turn, snarled.

"OK," Coach Laden said. "Rows of six. Hustle, don't walk. Line drill."

The whistle blew and the girls ran between lines on the court. Bending and touching. Sprinting back and forth, gutting it out until they reached the other end of the court. When Fat Angie's group ran, she finished last. Huffing-and-puffing last, but she did finish. Fat Angie was convinced that nothing short of having all appendages amputated could stop her.

The squad of hopefuls went through drill after drill. Dribbling techniques, passing, and, of course, defense. Given Fat Angie's girth along with her height, Coach Laden placed Fat Angie at post position, the position closest to the basketball hoop. In the middle of a play, Coach Laden called the Chicken Chat, a play designed by Laden with four possible executions depending on opposing team, score, and time on the clock.

Stacy Ann drove right for the bucket. Fat Angie slid right and planted her sneakers to avoid a foul. Stacy Ann slammed her to the ground for two — plus one Fat Angie knockdown point.

The whistle blew. Coach Laden marched into the circle of girls.

"What was that?" Coach Laden asked Stacy Ann.

"Come on, Coach," said Stacy Ann. "She doesn't belong out here. She can't even block."

Coach Laden, not looking as lovely as she might, leaned in to Stacy Ann. "So you're the coach now?"

Stacy Ann half-laughed, crossing her arms in defiance to save face with the girls.

"Did you play for the University of Tennessee? Do you have a national championship trophy encased for eternity?" asked Coach Laden. "I didn't think so. Angie, get up."

Coach Laden stepped back from the girls. "Set it up. I got all night."

Fat Angie scrambled to her feet. Stacy Ann scowled at her as she moved back into position.

From plays to basics, the girls practiced for hours. When Coach Laden whistled for a water break, Fat Angie stayed on the court. The girl was parched without a doubt, but she pulled the rack of basketballs onto the court and parked them near the free-throw line.

Coach Laden took notice of this act. Just as her mouth opened to call Fat Angie in for water, Fat Angie began what otherwise would seem unbelievable to anyone — except her sister. From one ball to the next, she power-shot free throws, missing not one of eleven in a row. When she got the last ball, she spun around the ball caddie, dribbled outside to the three-point arc, then pounded toward the key. Stopping hard, jumping straight up, form fiercely flawless, she sunk a beautiful jump shot.

She cheered, doing a dance best suited for the privacy of one's bedroom.

Fat Angie was not in her bedroom.

When she noticed the squad of hopefuls and a very lovely Coach Laden watching, she stopped in a not-so-flattering position. Regardless of her embarrassing dance, in that moment, Fat Angie was a dead ringer for her sister.

Coach Laden blew her whistle. "Jump shots. Line it up."

And so began Fat Angie's real bid for a place on the team.

Stacy Ann stood three girls behind Fat Angie and managed to be audible enough when she said, "What is this? Equal rights for freaks with dead sisters now?"

Fat Angie gritted her teeth. Coach Laden passed her the ball and blocked Fat Angie's path. That action in no way phased Fat Angie's forward motion as she dribbled, planted, and, with grace, nailed the jump shot.

Coach Laden shouted, "Next," watching Fat Angie jog to the back of the line.

When practice ended, Coach Laden had the girls collect the renegade basketballs. Coach Laden scooped one up and, tossing it at Fat Angie, simultaneously shouted, "Think fast!"

Again, fast responses were not Fat Angie's specialty.

The ball smashed into her nose.

The girls laughed.

This was not funny to Fat Angie.

"Locker room. Now," Coach Laden said to the girls.

Blood oozed out. Drip-dropping onto the famous yellow Hornet symbol center court. Fat Angie hated blood.

"Forward," Coach Laden said, holding out a towel. "Let me see. Well, it isn't broken."

Fat Angie stood awkwardly, feeling another "you're special" speech was imminent.

"You did good today," said Coach Laden.

"Thanks," said Fat Angie, her voice muffled by the towel.

"Your sister was really good at this game. I was surprised she turned down her scholarship," said Coach Laden. "She really loved it. Every second."

Fat Angie continued to bleed.

"Wanted to rid the world"—Fat Angie repositioned the towel—"of the tyranny of terrorism."

Coach Laden pulled the towel back and inspected the red puffiness that was Fat Angie's nose.

"Can you tell me why are you doing this, Angie?"

Fat Angie searched the recesses of her mind to come up with a stellar answer.

Fat Angie was short on stellar at that moment.

She exhaled from her mouth.

"This game . . . it's very competitive," said Coach Laden.

"I wanna play," said Fat Angie, removing the towel.

"What does your mom think?"

Fat Angie eased to the gym floor. Coach Laden followed.

"Doesn't it matter what *I* think?" said Fat Angie.

Coach Laden stretched her back with her palms flat on the floor. "I just think it's been a hard year. Don't you?"

Fat Angie crossed her legs, her sister's HORNETS' NEST T-shirt practically plastered to her wide wet torso.

"If you didn't know me or my sister—if you didn't know anything—would you give me a chance?"

"No."

This response stumped Fat Angie, who struggled to her feet. Her muscles tense and tired, she ambled toward the locker room.

"Angie," called Coach Laden. "See you tomorrow."

"But you just said—"

"I just said I *wouldn't* have given you a chance," said Coach Laden. "Go. And wash that shirt."

Fat Angie had stopped short of the locker room, to say

"thanks" or "super thanks," when she saw Coach Laden standing at the basketball caddie. She clutched the half-basketball charm and kissed it before resting it on her chest. It was not a religious symbol — as far as Fat Angie knew — but it was something she had never seen the coach without.

Coach Laden pushed the basketball caddie off the court and disappeared into the equipment room.

Fat Angie wanted to belong somewhere, to mean something to someone. She had meant the world and the intergalactic beyond to her sister.

"I was never alone when she was here. But, like, I'm in the room with other people now," Fat Angie had said to her therapist. *"People talking. Laughing. I dunno, I just . . . feel all weird."*

"Do you try to talk with anyone in these scenarios?"

"About what?" Fat Angie had asked.

"About themselves."

"But they'll lie. Everyone lies."

The therapist had made a note: *Paranoia could be symptomatic of psychotic tendencies.*

But KC had not been like everyone else. By and large, she was what one might call a straight shooter.

Through weeks of practicing with Jake, enduring the annoying ways of Wang, and consuming mass quantities of fresh fruit and leafy greens, Angie's determination to make the team had an echo of something purple. A purple heart and a pair of eighteen-eyehole combat boots. Fat Angie thought and thought, the nostalgia of the moment almost overwhelming her —

"Move it, Fatty," said a Stacy Ann minion, shoving past Angie from the locker room.

And just like that, Angie realized she had never been Fat Angie to KC. She had just been her. A smile erupted with no hesitation, and she knew what she had to do.

Chapter ELEVEN

Angie shivered. Her breath was shaped by the murky light streaming from the street and painting an outline of KC's porch. No sooner had Angie knocked than the neighbor's dog sparked from the darkness. His paws tore at the chain-link fence as he howled. The only thing holding him back was the rope tied to his collar tied to a tree.

Angie did not like this dog.

The dog most likely did not like Angie.

Angie growled at the dog.

The door opened. "Well, it's the famous Angie," said Esther, wiping paint from her hands.

"Famous?" asked Angie.

"Yeah, come on in. KC said you were trying out for the varsity basketball team. Trying makes you famous to me."

"Hey," said a guy, kissing Esther. "Pizza's coming."

Angie wrote a mental Post-it of what appeared to be a fifteen-year age difference, give or take a year or two.

"Angie, this is Mike," said Esther.

"Hey," he said, holding out his paint-smudged hand. "I knew your sister."

The past tense of the statement forced Angie into a polite halfhearted smile.

"Great gal, her sister," said Mike to Esther. "She'd rock this town on a Friday night the way they do football down in Texas."

"KC didn't mention you had a sister," said Esther. "She off to college?"

"She's in the air force. She's fighting—in Iraq. Yup."

Mike, like everyone else in Dryfalls, knew that Angie's sister was not fighting in the war. But unlike many people, he did not say a single word to the contrary. He simply smiled.

"I'm not much for the war, but I support the troops," said Esther.

"Hey," said KC, popping iBuds out of her ears as she stepped out of her bedroom.

Mike immediately put distance between Esther and himself.

"I'm gonna get back to painting," Mike said. "Good to hear you're trying to rock the board, Angie. Town needs a good run again."

"Angie just stopped in," Esther said to KC.

"Esther, I'm not blind."

"OK. I'm just the mom . . . who's gonna let you paint

your room Buzz Lightyear Blue and Rebel Raw Red," Esther said, approaching KC. "Give her a break. She's a sweet girl."

"Esther . . ."

"And quit listening to Death Cab for Cutie," Esther said. "It makes you too depressed."

"Relax, it's retro night with Jewel. Nothing but slit-the-wrists tracks," said KC.

"Not funny," Esther said. "Never funny, KC."

Esther had never taken a serious tone with KC. Clearly this was not a moot point.

"OK," KC said. "Don't break a spring."

"Dinner will be here in half an hour."

"Mike's idea?" KC said.

"He's nice," Esther said.

"He's twelve."

"Only in dog years."

"Yeah, well, I'm kinda sick of pizza," KC said.

Beat.

"He didn't call," Esther said. "Do you want me to call him? 'Cause I will, honey."

"I *don't* wanna get into it."

Esther nodded.

Angie's eyes circled the room in the hope of finding something interesting to land on. At that moment, it was a copy of *Time* magazine with Steve Jobs on the cover. He had died.

That had not been what she wanted to land on.

"Well, I'll let'cha know when dinner gets here," Esther said. "Good to see you again, Angie."

Angie stood, uncomfortably comfortable. A strange double mood she had mastered out of the necessity of avoiding confrontation.

KC hung against the wall. "What are you doing here?"

"Um . . ." Angie started counting in her head and finished out loud with eight, nine, and ten.

She died 1000.2 deaths every second KC said nothing. What was there to say? To do? Clearly, the space wedged between them was thick.

KC had peeled off the wall and was halfway to her bedroom when she looked over her shoulder. Angie was cemented in place.

"Come on," KC said.

Angie followed four and a half steps behind KC to KC's room. Something was different. Something she was not able to decipher in the brief time from entrance to KC saying, "What are you doing here?"

KC fell back on her bed and reached for a graphic novel.

Fat Angie dipped her head and bit the inside of her cheek.

She had told her therapist, *"I suck. I hate who I am."*

The therapist had made a note: *Cognitive dissonance.*

"Esther said you knew about tryouts," said Fat Angie.

"I was walking by." KC flipped the page.

"Oh. I thought maybe . . ." Fat Angie stretched her neck to one side. Then the other. "Maybe we could . . . hang out? See, my mom's over at Wang's therapist's tonight. We could spy on her and, um . . . take some pictures for your Wall of Weird So Twisted."

"That's a little dark," said KC, still reading. "Even for the wall."

"Yeah, I thought so too. Um . . . I was just kidding about the spying picture thing."

Only she had not been kidding. Not entirely. Like most kids, Angie did not relish the thought of seeing her mother in lip-to-lip passion with Wang's court-appointed therapist. But some part of her wondered what it would be like to see her mother care about someone . . . have affection for a person who was not herself. Angie's father had wondered the same thing about his wife, according to deposition transcripts Angie had acquired by accident on purpose.

"So, that's it?" KC asked, not looking up from her graphic novel.

"No." Fat Angie cleared her throat. "I didn't want you to go the other day. It wasn't the other day. It was, um . . . a lot of days ago."

"Weeks," added KC.

"Yeah. When we were standing there and talking and almost . . . well, what I think we were gonna . . . and you touched my scars and I wanted . . . I didn't want you to go."

"Yet I did," said KC. "That's the mystery of the new mystery girl. She always has the uncanny ability to vanish without anyone noticing."

"I noticed," said Fat Angie.

"Like you've noticed me at lunch or in the hallways or at gym?" KC asked.

"I didn't know what to . . . say."

"Uh, 'Hey' works," KC said. "Or 'Wanna lunch?' "

"I'm not cool like that. I'm Fat Angie. I mean, I'm —"

KC softened slightly. As she laid down her graphic novel, her hair fell away, revealing the purple heart. Fat Angie's own heart went aflutter.

"Look, seeing you on *Dateline* aside, I don't know," said KC. "From the moment I saw you in gym, it just seemed . . ."

"Yeah."

"Yeah," said KC. "But it's way more complicated than just . . . *yeah.*"

"Yeah," said Fat Angie, brow quite furrowed.

KC sat up, adjusting her peace-sign belt buckle.

"That's a swell buckle," said Fat Angie.

"Thanks," KC said, a smirk capturing the essence of her face. "My dad. Technically his secretary, but technicalities are stupid sometimes."

"My dad does that too. I'm mean, he gets his new wife to do it. She'll give me anything. There's a good chance I'll get a pony for Christmas."

The girls laughed.

"I don't even want a pony. It was a joke," Fat Angie said.

"Look," said KC. "Let's bypass all the heavy-strange-we-don't-know-how-to-act-around-each-other thing and go do something pseudodangerous and fun."

Fat Angie nodded.

KC grabbed her fitted leather coat and was halfway out her bedroom window when Fat Angie said, "Why are we going out the window?"

"I don't know. Seemed different. More dangerous."

Fat Angie followed, her exit lacking grace.

The neighbor's dog burst into a rampage. Fat Angie backed against the house.

KC threw a handful of Chex Mix that scattered like buckshot into the dog's yard.

"No worries. He's just lonely," KC said. "So, lead the way."

"Where?"

"To Wang's head shrinker's Den of Sin."

"Seriously?" asked Fat Angie, a pop of glee in her voice.

"Absolute."

A cool breeze blew past them.

"You ever get that feeling?" asked KC. "When you know something big is right around the corner? The wind whips up and the sky clears just enough for you to see a pocketful of stars —"

"And one of them seems like it's winking at you," Fat Angie said.

"Yeah," KC said. "And just like that, it all feels like it's gonna line right up. The way I see it, Angie, you and me are like Thelma and Louise, like Buffy and Willow, like . . ."

"KC and Angie."

"Yeah. Just like that."

There was no turning back. Especially as they stood outside of Wang's therapist's house. Fat Angie's couldn't-be-bothered mother's leased gas-guzzling vehicle sat in the modest driveway.

"Did you hear that?" whispered Fat Angie, looking behind her.

The spray of a street lamp caught the shadow of a figure in a hoodie.

"Come on," KC whispered back, tugging on Fat Angie's elbow. "It's nothing."

Fat Angie was sure it was *not* nothing. It looked like *something*. But they were midway across the lawn and ducked into the not-so-well-trimmed bushes before she could get a closer look.

Fat Angie and KC held the ledge to Wang's therapist's window. The two girls watched Fat Angie's couldn't-be-bothered mother, Connie, curl up on a dark pleather sofa. Muffled jazz music muted what Angie thought had to be a mundane monologue, as her mother's lips were in constant movement.

"Don't you feel kinda like Cagney and Lacey on a stake-out?" KC said quietly.

"You know *Cagney and Lacey*?" said Fat Angie.

"Yeah . . . hot cop and mom cop paving the way for women on TV. Totally retro feminist. There would be no *Buffy the Vampire Slayer* without *Cagney and Lacey.* And trust me, the world is a better place with *BTVS.*"

The shrub rustled behind them.

It was the nothing. Now a definite something. Fat Angie held her breath when—

"Hey," said Jake. "What are you doing?"

"What are *you* doing?" asked Fat Angie.

"Shh . . ." said KC.

"I saw you up on Main," Jake whispered. "Didn't you hear me?"

"No," said Fat Angie.

Jake threw a disapproving look at KC, who did not seem to care.

"Well, how did it go at tryouts?" he asked Angie. "Thought you were gonna text."

KC grabbed Fat Angie's hand. "She was golden. Absolute."

Fat Angie had not shared the experience with any detail to KC and was consequently confused by her praise. And the hand-holding.

"Yeah," said Jake, eyes on KC's sudden cling to Fat

Angie's hand. "And you're hiding in somebody's bushes *why?*"

"Thought I'd take some candid photos of my mom making fun with Wang's court-appointed therapist. Just in case she ever threatens to institutionalize me again."

"That's a little dark," said Jake.

"That's what *I* said," KC affirmed. "Relax. She's using my cell and is under strict orders *not* to photograph any nudies."

Jake pushed up along the wall and looked in the window.

The therapist and Angie's couldn't-be-bothered mother were engaged in first-base making out.

"Your mom really is a steam."

Both girls grimaced.

"What?" asked Jake. "Moms can be hot."

"If you're a freak," Fat Angie whispered.

"Anyway, let's go to The Backstory. I mean, if you're done with the peeping creeper routine."

Fat Angie shrugged. "I'm not exactly Backstory material."

"Says who? Gary? Stacy Ann? You can't expect people to know you if you're always running from them," said Jake.

"She said she didn't wanna go," KC said.

"She can *speak* for herself," said Jake.

"Not with you thinking for her," KC said.

"Whoa," said Fat Angie. "Remember, still here."

Jake shook his head and squat-walked along the edge of the bush.

"Jake . . ." Fat Angie squat-walked behind him.

"What is this?" he whispered. "This spy-girl thing. Was it her idea?"

"No. It was mine."

Jake shook his head. "It doesn't seem like an Angie idea."

"Well, maybe I have . . . Angie ideas you don't know about. Besides, I like her, Jake. I told you that. You seemed kinda cool with it and now you're being all weird-big-brother?"

Jake scratched his head and looked down. He clearly was hiding something.

"If you change your mind, kick me a text," said Jake. "I'll meet you at the door."

Fat Angie crawled back to KC and propped herself against the cheap siding. "He didn't mean anything."

"It's just a guy thing," KC said.

"Jake's not a guy thing. What I mean is . . . he's different. He practices with me every day. When he could be with his friends. He's really OK."

The girls quietly chomped on bits of Chex Mix that KC had retrieved from her jacket. A new version of awkward crept between them and the creeping vine on the shrub. A classic tune from the multi-award-winning group Chicago seeped through the edges of Wang's therapist's window. It set a mood of tentative romance for Fat Angie and KC. It had been approximately twenty-one days, eighteen hours, and seven minutes since they had openly in closed quarters admitted they were gay-girl gay with each other.

Fat Angie's cumbersome first move of hand-to-knee contact with KC edged the moment into supreme geekness. Fat Angie took a gulp of gulp and tried not to tremble.

"Hey," said KC, tipping her head toward Fat Angie.

"Yeah," Fat Angie said, staring at her untied shoe.

She shifted forward and tied it. Double knots . . . like her stomach. When she pushed back against the wall, KC had mysteriously edged closer. KC leaned in, her luscious lips parting, and . . .

"I once kissed a guy with a prosthetic leg," said Fat Angie.

This phrase definitely threw a wrench in the Chicago-fueled mood.

"Really?" KC asked.

"No," said Fat Angie. "Just his picture from the Special Olympics article I tore out of a magazine in my dentist's office."

KC grinned. "Cool."

She leaned forward again.

"You know . . ." said Fat Angie, turning away.

KC grabbed the girl's chin midturn and pulled her in.

The kiss was . . . disastrous.

Fat Angie had no idea what to do. This was not like her experience of kissing the prosthetic boy's photograph. This was real lips and real tongue and real scary.

Their lips remained in strained smushed position for approximately seven seconds.

KC pulled back, her fingertips pressed to her cherry ChapStick lips.

"Wow," KC said. "That sucked."

Fat Angie shriveled in place.

"It sucked for you, right?" said KC.

"Oh, yeah," Fat Angie said, unsure if playing it nonchalant was standard first-kiss protocol. Surely it wasn't KC's first kiss. Surely KC knew it had been hers.

"I'm usually . . . I mean, wow," said KC.

"Oh, me too. Usually," said Fat Angie.

"Usually what?" asked KC.

"Usually, um . . ." Fat Angie searched the recesses of her brain. Nothing but a vacancy sign blinked in the immediate foreground of her thought process. "Do you wanna block out our caller ID and crank call Stacy Ann?"

"Cool," said KC, scratching at her fitted black long-sleeved T-shirt with a portrait of Gandhi on the chest.

Fat Angie caught a glimpse of KC's arms. The scratches . . . scars.

"You OK?" said Fat Angie.

"Yeah. Relax. I told you I'm over that. It's so ancient. Like the miniseries as an art form."

KC casually tugged her sleeve into her palm and scooted closer to Fat Angie. Angie tingled when KC's shirt brushed against her forearm.

"I'm gonna crank my dad," said KC.

"Yeah. Oh, and then my mom."

"That'll killjoy the romance," KC said.

"No doubt. Ultra joykill."

Fat Angie had no doubt repackaged the word. Much to Angie's chagrin, KC surprised her when she said, "Sweet word twist. *Joykill* rocks."

And this was an absolutely swell moment.

"Crank on?" Angie said.

The girls fiercely dialed one number after another. Pissing off a string of unhappy answerers.

KC hung up on her dad and, floating on the high, leaned in and kissed Angie. This time, Angie recalled the upside-down Spider-Man movie kiss that had been her fantasy study guide for kissing, and she kissed back!

The two girls came up for a breather and touched heads.

"That *so* didn't—" said KC.

"Yeah, so didn't," said Fat Angie.

"Wanna . . . ?" asked KC.

"Yeah . . ."

When the girls resumed their smooch, there was a sound. A snap-of-a-twig sound.

Fat Angie paused. "Did you hear . . . ?"

"What?"

Fat Angie did not want to be paranoid. Especially right then.

She had told her therapist, *"Everyone thinks I'm paranoid. What if they're paranoid and are projecting?"*

The therapist had made a note: *Struggling with social norms in relation to adulthood.*

"Angie," said KC.

"It's nothing," Fat Angie said.

KC asked, "You freaking?"

"No. I mean, it's . . . different?" said Angie. "Not bad different."

"Definitely?" asked KC.

"Absolute," said Angie.

The two leaned toward each other.

"KC?"

"Yeah, Angie?"

Angie. Her name fit her when KC said it. It was the perfect size.

"Nothing."

The smoochfest was a breath from resuming when the door to Wang's therapist's house whipped open. Fat Angie and KC peeked out from beneath the bottom of the bush.

A pair of sneakers sprinting from grass to concrete was muffled by the clicking of her mother's high heels.

"Come back in, Connie," said the therapist. "It's not that big of a deal."

Her couldn't-be-bothered mother abruptly got in her car and sped out of the driveway.

"Wonder what we missed," KC said.

Fat Angie shook her head. "I better go."

"Hey," said KC. "You OK?"

"I'm fine. But if she's heading home, I better be there."

Fat Angie made to leave but veered back to KC. "The kissing thing."

"Yeah?"

"You think we could try that again?" Fat Angie said. "Maybe soon sometime?"

"Definitely soonish," KC said.

From ear to beautiful ear, Fat Angie grin-glowed.

"Text me," KC said.

"Right. I gotta go. Bye. Thanks, I mean." Fat Angie stumbled out from beneath the hedge.

She sprinted though her sore muscles said, "Briskly walk, please." She ran on the taste of her first kiss with the luscious KC Romance.

Chapter TWELVE

The girl *huffed.*

The girl *puffed.*

The girl, in Fat Angie–style, barreled through the front door.

Fat Angie's couldn't-be-bothered mother said, "Where have you been?" The shrillness in her voice should have blown the girl right down.

"Thought you were working late," Fat Angie said, catching her breath.

Wang strolled in, popped a Coke, and poured a packet of Pop Rocks in his mouth. He gargled the mixture. This was an annoying distraction to Fat Angie.

"I asked you where you were, Angie," said her mother.

The tension in her mother's voice confused her.

"I was, um, out."

Wang stuck out his tongue, Pop Rocks crackling. Fat Angie glared at him. He glared back. They were in a free-for-all glare-off that could have continued for quite some time if—

"Where were you?" her mother asked.

"Nowhere," said Fat Angie. "Why don't you ask him where he was?"

"I knew you'd start again," said her mother. "It always has to be something big with you, Angie."

Fat Angie knew this was more than just being busted for coming in after 11:30 on a school night. It had to be about tryouts.

"Look, I really want to do this," Fat Angie said.

"You what?" snapped her mother.

"Try it . . . for a while," said Fat Angie. "It feels right—like maybe it's who I am. Can't you just support me?"

Her mother unhooked her cell phone from the harness.

"Mom, I'm really good at—"

But before Fat Angie could finish talking about basketball tryouts, her jaw dropped.

Her chin doubled.

A fly could have nested in her mouth.

Right there in dimly lit but high resolution on her mother's BlackBerry was a picture of KC and Fat Angie in full lip-lock action. This was very, very bad.

"I sent it to your father," said her mother. "Not that he'll do a damn thing."

Fat Angie's jaw was still dropped.

Her chin remained doubled.

Wang leaned over his mother's shoulder and chuckled.

"Way to go, deep-fried," said Wang.

This did not please his mother.

"How? Where . . . did this . . . ?" Fat Angie asked.

"There is always someone watching us, Angie," said her mother. "My God. You want me to support you doing this?"

"No . . ." said Fat Angie. "I meant . . . what I was talking about . . . I wasn't talking about *that.*"

"I don't care what you were talking about," said her mother.

"Mom —"

"The only thing I can ever imagine supporting you in is a genuine attempt at losing weight," said her mother.

"What?" said Fat Angie.

"Don't think I don't know you sneak food," said her mother.

Fat Angie covered her belly. Wang's interest in the showdown between mother and obese sister diminished with the need to text.

"There's nothing you won't pull, is there?" her mother asked. "Nothing you won't *do* to make us the freak show of the neighborhood. Of Dryfalls."

"Don't you have that in reverse?" said Fat Angie.

"Why, because I want to get on with our lives?" asked her mother.

Connie + Get On With Life = Accept Angie's Sister Is Dead

Fat Angie's sister was *not* dead.

Her body had *not* been found.

Fat Angie's cotton socks stuck to —

"Answer me." Fat Angie did not like confrontation. She especially didn't like confrontation with her mother.

"I don't want you talking to this girl ever again."

"What?" Fat Angie asked.

Wang cut in. "She said you can't lock lesbo lips with the —"

"Shut up, rice muncher," Fat Angie said.

"Fatty Acid —"

"Enough!" said their mother, turning to Wang. "You will *go* to therapy or no more cell phone or computer."

"I don't care," Wang said, slipping his cell in his jeans pocket.

"If you don't go, the court has the very real option of taking you out of this house. Is that what you want?" said Fat Angie's mother.

She held her place, toe-to-toe with her adopted son. They were both five foot nine and of a similar build.

He scratched the end of his nose, made a you've-got-me-pinned face, and looked away. Defeating Wang had not simmered the explosion that was Connie as she turned back to her daughter.

"No more girls with tattoos," Fat Angie's mother said.

"No more *anything*. You will do whatever it takes to be normal again."

Fat Angie looked to Wang to say something—anything—from his arsenal of piss-Mom-off comments. He rubbed the end of his peach-fuzzed chin and offered nothing in the way of a distraction.

"This isn't . . ." Fat Angie shook her head, breathing deep. "You're never—when do you . . . even *care* what we do? You're never . . . *here.*"

Wang sipped his Coke. Fat Angie took note because she was unusually thirsty.

"Listen. This is not a democracy. You will *do* what I say," warned her mother.

"No," Fat Angie said, her voice not filled with the confidence it needed.

Fat Angie's mother got in her daughter's grill.

"You will not shame me again," said her mother. "This picture is *sick.*"

Fat Angie shook her head, an almost uncontrollable gesture.

"I am not *sick*. I am—"

Fat Angie's mother hooked her by the elbow. "Mom . . . ouch!" Fat Angie said, completely surprised by her mother's monster grip.

She dragged Fat Angie down the hall, past the framed photographs of Fat Angie's once perfectly posed family.

"Mom, stop!" squealed Fat Angie.

Wang followed behind them. "Mom, cut it out," he said.

Her mother trampled through piles of dirty laundry and paperback novels on Fat Angie's floor, a pigsty the girl referred to as "in a state of constant change."

"Let's look," said her mother, tearing a collage of clippings, mostly about Fat Angie's sister's disappearance, off the closet mirror. "Let's see the real you."

Her mother crumpled the newspaper page featuring Fat Angie's sister winning the state championship and the color printout of the first beagle to win best in show.

"Mom," said Wang, pulling at Connie. She shoved him back.

"Look," said her mother, forcing Fat Angie in front of the mirror.

Her mother turned Fat Angie's wrists out, yanked off her Casio calculator watch, and revealed the scars of her attempted suicide.

"Look at them," said her mother. "Look at you!"

Tears ran down the girl's flushed face. Despite the weeks of training with Jake and the leafy greens, she saw that she was still big enough to be ugly. Scarred enough to be crazy.

Fat Angie saw Wang's reflection in the mirror. Wang was not smiling. He was not grinning in the least.

"You *are* sick," her mother continued, squeezing Fat Angie's fat roll. "And you're fat."

Fat Angie sobbed in a big way.

"At least your sister tried to do something with her life. She died doing something—"

"Shut up! Shut up! Shut up!" Fat Angie cupped her hands over her ears.

Her mother yanked her hands away. "You play crazy all you want in these four walls. You play your little game. But it stops when you go out that door. You hear me? I won't have it anymore, Angie. I won't."

Fat Angie began to count in her head. She had to calm down. Shut down. Cool down. *Don't react,* she thought. *Don't scream. Don't make so much as a move. Don't let* her *know she has reached inside and strangled your heart. Just don't even try to breathe.*

When Fat Angie opened her eyes, her mother was gone. Only she and Wang were reflected in the mirror. Him noodle-skinny and her undeniably fat.

"You OK?" Wang asked.

"Just leave." Fat Angie's lip trembled.

Fat Angie had revealed to her therapist, *"I miss how Wang was. It was different when she was here. She was this sticky glue. She knew how to keep us all together. Not like people who have babies to stay together. That's stupid. You know?"*

The therapist had made a note: *Fantasizes about birthing rituals.*

The sound of Wang's overpriced in-style boots clunked down the hall and disappeared behind his bedroom door. An Italian cooking show blared from his room.

Wang did not speak Italian.

Wang did not like to cook.

Fat Angie's cell phone beeped. KC had texted, U cool?

Fat Angie looked out her *Pretty in Pink* curtains. Jake was at his computer, not at The Backstory. Fat Angie went from devastated to full-throttle angry in zero-to-hero speed. Jake had taken the picture. Jake had set her up. He hated KC. He had never cared for Fat Angie.

Chapter THIRTEEN

The next morning Fat Angie walked through the halls of William Anders High as the center attraction. The picture of her and KC had gone miniviral and was all anyone could talk about. She stopped short of her locker. Plastered in laser color copy was the pic of the two girls lip-locked with the words WACKO DYKE in red across the top. In that moment, Fat Angie's life had finally reached the equivalent of Carrie's with the gym class throwing tampons at her. Only she did not have the likes of Stephen King scripting her a cool telekinetic power.

None of that mattered. Her so-called life as a crazy fatso was over. This one moment, captured in high-resolution digital quality, would be the nail in her coffin, she thought. People might forget crazy. They might even forgive fat. But *dyke.* Throw that into the teen mix of conservative Dryfalls, Ohio, and there would be no escape.

Hushed giggles surrounded her.

Smirks spread like swine flu.

Kids elbowed one another.

Fat Angie ripped the image off her locker and sprinted, at Fat Angie speed, to the gym. She flew past Wang's friends, who oinked in unison. Wang reluctantly followed her.

"Angie," Wang said, grabbing hold of her arm.

"Leave me alone," she said, wiggling from his grip.

Down the hall. Past a cell-phone snapshot and a video geek chasing her with a handheld camera, she ran. Shouldering a door and cutting across the school yard, she made for the gym.

Catching her breath, Fat Angie stood with her hands pressed against the gymnasium trophy case. The picture that had frequented the news the most. Her sister wore an All-State medal around her neck and clutched the state trophy in her arms. Everything had been in front of her. A scholarship. A college of significant stature. And she had chosen camouflage and artillery. She had chosen the world over all of those things and, most important, over Fat Angie.

Now her sister was just a face behind a recently Windex-washed case. Spotless and held in time, forever smiling. Fat Angie opened the crumpled color printout from her locker. That was the happiest she had been since her sister—the happiest ever, maybe. She was not sure. No. Of course she was sure. It had been her happiest personal moment with someone who was not her sister. Right then, happy seemed more than wrong. It seemed sick. Like all the thoughts in her head.

Fat Angie's cell phone beeped. A text from KC read, Where R U?

She turned her cell phone off and stuffed it into her tight tattered back pocket. The notion of hiding was extremely appealing; however, she would have to attend the second and final day of basketball tryouts to vie for a spot on the team.

The pressure was too great.

She stared at her sneaker toe.

She scrunched her face tight.

She—

"Angie," Coach Laden called from down the hall. "You OK?"

"Umm . . ." said Fat Angie. "Yeah."

Fat Angie unclenched her face.

"You sure?" said Coach Laden.

Fat Angie was hesitant to reveal any information that might bar her from the team.

"Coach Laden. If you . . ." Fat Angie worked to say the words. "If you were different . . . would that make you sick?"

She had asked that very question of her therapist, who had replied, *"Why would you want to be different?"*

Fat Angie had elected not to speak for the remaining fourteen minutes of the session.

The therapist had made a note: *Struggles with notions of community.*

Coach Laden motioned Fat Angie toward her office. Reluctantly, Fat Angie lagged toward the sacred Mecca of championship headlines and dense playbooks. A framed newspaper clipping of Fat Angie's sister was the centerpiece of the office.

Coach Laden sat behind her desk and popped the lid off her steaming coffee. "What's up?"

"Um . . ." Fat Angie sighed. "Is it normal to wonder? Wonder what you're supposed to be?"

"Sure," said Coach Laden. "It's what we do our whole lives."

"That's kinda extreme," said Fat Angie.

Coach Laden grinned. "Except, we substitute the 'supposed to' with 'who we are.' Right then. That's what defines an exceptional person. Like you."

"I told you, I'm not special," said Fat Angie, her tone distinctly on guard.

"Hey, I didn't say special," said Coach Laden, leaning on her elbows. "I said exceptional."

The word *exceptional* had never been used in reference to Fat Angie. After her sister had joined the armed forces, after the divorce, and after her sister's highly publicized disappearance, Fat Angie had been reminded how "special" she was. But it was said through so much politeness, so false and insincere. While fighting against the "special," another part of her had started to believe it. Believe that she was "special" and had to be protected from the world and everyone in it.

She found this to be incredibly lonely.

"Angie, I know it's not easy for you," said Coach Laden. "For a lot of reasons."

"Definitely a lot."

"But you don't quit," said Coach Laden. "That's a stand-out trait."

Uneasy, Fat Angie arched her back. "I tried to kill myself in front of hundreds of people and several local networks. Trust me, that's quitting in my family."

"That's not quitting," said Coach Laden, sipping her coffee. "Quitting would have been if you had stayed in the bathroom. You didn't want to quit. Right?"

Of course, she had not wanted to die. Suicide, as some might say, would have sucked! Still, Angie had not wanted to live, especially thinking that her sister was dead.

"Angie, I'm not a therapist, OK?" said Coach Laden. "And maybe you'd be better off talking to the guidance counselor than me."

"Doubtful," Fat Angie said.

"You don't try to be anyone else and that is a very hard thing in this world. It may seem unimportant right now when fitting in would be so much easier. But later you'll see. Being who you are is everything."

Fat Angie did not know who to be. Not from one moment to the next, as if every path were paved with eggshells.

"Angie?" said Coach Laden. "See you at tryouts, right?"

"Yeah," she said, biting the inside of her cheek.

With her shoulders dropped forward, she hauled herself out the door and resumed her place at the trophy case, her forehead pressed against the glass. When she exhaled, the glass steamed. She wiped it away and there was her sister smiling back at her.

Fat Angie did not want to go to class. However, she would have to suck it up because her sister would be home soon. She was quite certain about that and she simply could not quit. That was one thing her sister never did. She never ever quit.

Fat Angie sat in the cafeteria with the usual seven empty seats surrounding her. She had opted for the vegetarian lunch, referred to as Pop and Energy. She eyed the iceberg lettuce with overly processed cheese.

Gary Klein, a couple of tables away, flicked his tongue wildly between the triangle of his fingers and thumbs.

Jake parted through a crowd and strutted toward her. He played it high-school cool, sitting at the end of the table with his back to her.

"What do you want?" said Fat Angie.

Jake half-smiled to a group of girls watching from the food line.

"What were you thinking letting KC take that picture?" said Jake.

"What are you talking about?" Fat Angie slammed her chair back, crashing it into the guy sitting behind her. "*You* took that picture."

"What?" Jake said, facing her.

"You've been part of some get-the-wacko-fat-freak plan, haven't you?" she asked. "Admit it. Stacy Ann put you up to this whole do-gooder, I-care-about-Angie crap."

"OK, I loathe Stacy Ann, for starters. And I didn't take that picture," said Jake.

"Right. You're the only one who knew I was there," said Fat Angie. "You think Stacy Ann is so pissed at me that she's tagged me with a tracking device?"

The two paused to consider the probability of that statement. Improbable.

"I mean, you just showed up," said Fat Angie.

Jake squirmed. Squirmed in the sense of shifting his weight from one leg to the other and jamming his hands in his front baggy jeans pockets.

"Why would I help you practice every day after school for weeks — taking crap from my parents? My friends?" said Jake.

"Your life must be so difficult now."

"Will you stop it?" Jake said. "Just stop attacking me for fitting in."

Jake dropped his head. He seemed to be in a dilemma as to what to say.

"I promised your sister, OK?" Jake said. "If something ever . . . happened to her, I'd show. For you. But then I messed it all up. I knew, even before the whole suicide thing. I knew you were in trouble. I just . . ."

Fat Angie glared at him. She was becoming quite talented at glaring.

"Look, I don't come from a family with all kinds of weird sadness. I'm not so good at—I totally screwed it all up, all right?"

Pause.

"But I didn't mean to," Jake said. "And I've been trying—"

"To get rid of your guilt?" said Fat Angie. "Because you were just like the rest of them before?"

"I was never like them," Jake said. *"Never."*

"Someone took that picture," Fat Angie said.

"Hey," KC said, coming up behind Angie. "Where have you been?"

Angie put distance between herself and KC. She thought that would somehow erase the image of their impassioned kiss from the minds of the cafeteria kids.

"Look, I didn't take that picture," said Jake. "I'm not like that. I wouldn't hurt you."

"You're a jock," said Fat Angie. "You suddenly care because of some alleged promise."

"I. Didn't. Do. It," he said.

"OK" said KC. "Everyone, cool your jets. First, Angie, you're acting like an ass. You haven't texted me once. That is grade A bad form. And second, though it's unbelievable to me, Jack didn't take the pic."

"Jake," he said.

"Whatever," said KC. "Apparently, Wang's ex-girlfriend told a girl in my history class who passed a note that I intercepted . . . your brother's the origin. He snapped the pic and made it go viral."

Fat Angie was stun gunned. "He acted so concerned. . . . Of course. We both knew where Mom was."

"So what?" said KC, reaching for Angie's hand. "We'll fight viral with badass coolness."

"It's a big *so,*" said Fat Angie, pulling back.

Jake dipped his head. "This isn't San Francisco, KC. Dryfalls, Ohio, isn't exactly rainbow friendly."

"And you're the designated go-to guy about all things oppressive?" said KC.

"Hey, I've seen kids get hurt. Taunted and pushed around. I've seen what they do to Angie just for being herself without you —"

"Shut up!" said Fat Angie. "OK? I'm not invisible."

"Good job on scoring the dyke vote for student council this year," a guy said, walking past Jake.

Jake looked at the two girls. The awkward heavy pause planted itself among them.

"KC, I'm not . . . pretty. I'm not . . . *normal,*" said Fat Angie. "This just gives everyone something else to stack against me. And I've gotta make the team. This is so important to me."

"So being with me . . . like, that—that's what?" KC said.

Fat Angie did not take the necessary time needed to think through all the possible responses. She was under the gun. At least in her mind.

"I made a mistake, OK?" said Fat Angie.

KC nodded. "Mistake. Hmm. Wow."

Fat Angie's heart was 199.5 percent breaking. And while that estimate felt unbearable and possibly not properly equated, she said, "I'm sorry."

"Yeah, me too." KC leaned in to Fat Angie. "You break it. You know? My heart."

Fat Angie's eyes fell to the purple heart tattoo on KC's neck.

"I thought you were different," said KC, walking away. "Good luck. Assimilating."

Fat Angie stood with her stomach protruding over her jeans. Watching KC become smaller and smaller as she stepped out the glass double doors into the courtyard.

"Angie, we can fix this," said Jake. "I think."

Fat Angie's eyes shot left, then right. In a film, the camera would have circled around her as she searched for one thing: Wang.

Wang's friends motioned at the dark-haired fury closing in with venomous rage. He lowered his head and pretended that he was involved in the pointless chatter of his under-achieving friends.

Wang forgot the most important rule in war:

Never take your eyes off your opponent.

Fat Angie cracked Wang over the head with her plastic tray. Lettuce and fat-free milk rained onto the table, pears and cutlery slap-clanging to the floor.

"What the hell are you doing, freak?" said Wang, backing away from her.

Fat Angie continued to pummel him with the tray.

Whack! Smack! Whack-whack!

He threw up his arms, blocking his head.

"You sent out that picture," said Fat Angie. "Why?"

"I don't know what you're talking about. I didn't send anything."

She backed him against the wall, her eyes burning an imaginary hole in his skull.

"Don't lie!" she said.

Her exclamation dialed down the general volume of the lunchroom.

Jake stepped in behind her.

"Look, I'm sorry," Wang said. "It was supposed to be a joke."

Fat Angie had eavesdropped on a conversation between her couldn't-be-bothered mother and Wang's court-appointed therapist, who had said, "There are so many layers to his trauma, Connie. His sense of abandonment from his birth family and your divorce has resulted in what we refer to as invisible angry teen syndrome (IATS). While not a formal medical diagnosis, IATS is a very real syndrome. They have done studies in Luxembourg on rats. It's very new material but very promising."

"A joke?" Fat Angie said.

Wang's school tough-cool intensity fell away. "It was just . . . I didn't think—I didn't think," said Wang.

She nodded.

"Nothing you ever did up until now made me hate you," said Fat Angie. "Because I think you miss her too. That's why you're such an ass all the time. But I don't care anymore." She pushed in. "I hate you."

"Come on," said Jake.

Fat Angie had shot and scored from the three-point line, metaphorically speaking. Wang had shared with Angie over a video-game marathon of *Donkey Kong* that his birth father had said those three words to him before forcing his mother to send him away. In the heat of the moment, she had deliberately wounded Wang and she did not care.

"Angie," said Jake.

Her eyes held to Wang's as she stepped back.

Wang hooked Jake by the arm. "You're a fake, Jake. Whatever you're doing with my sister, you're worse than me."

Jake jerked his arm away.

As Jake and Fat Angie walked to the cafeteria doors, kids laughed. Some hollered. Some even booed. The name-calling specifics were insignificant. And in that moment, Angie just did not care. That scared her.

When the last bell rang, Fat Angie cut out through an emergency exit that did, in fact, sound. She ran as fast as she could and plowed into the girls' locker room. Huffing, she pulled her sister's HORNETS' NEST T-shirt from the bottom of her backpack. It was carefully protected in an oversize Ziploc freezer bag. She gathered her clothes and changed in a stall. This action often made her feel much like Clark Kent changing from mere mortal to Superman. Today, however, she was feeling much less the super and more the Clark. Even with her sister's shirt on.

Her fingers hooked the latch when the locker room filled with laughter and girl gossip. She squatted with her feet planted on the toilet seat.

"Who took my water bottle?" a girl whined.

"Ask Keisha. She's always five-finger-discounting my shit."

"Don't make me get all brick on you, chicken legs," said Keisha.

"OK, OK. Best scandal of the year," said Stacy Ann. "Head cheerleader Amber 'Precious' Pom-Pom Hiller knocked up by D-list woodshop junior DeMel Allen, or . . ."

Stacy Ann paused. The tension must have swelled. Fat Angie's foot slipped momentarily. She recovered quickly, bracing herself against the stall walls, but fumbled her clothes right into the toilet. The toilet that had not been flushed.

"Man . . ." she whispered.

"Or Fat Angie slitting her wrist and going lesbo?" asked Stacy Ann.

One of Stacy Ann's clan made a buzzer sound. "I'll take Wacko Fatso Dyke for five hundred bonus points, please."

The girls laughed.

"Cut it out," said a girl. "She might make the team."

Fat Angie tried to fish her clothes out of the toilet without drawing attention to the only occupied stall.

"Yeah, only because Coach Laden is a complete card-carrying dyke," said Stacy Ann.

That statement paused Fat Angie's clothing retrieval. Coach Laden a lesbian? No way. She was so . . . lovely. But so was KC. That was when KC's initials bore a hole into Fat Angie's gut. What had she been thinking at lunch? KC was the only person to see Angie for who she was and not treat her like Kryptonite.

Fat Angie's shoe slipped. In less than a second, she slid, sneaker-first, into the toilet. The water splashed out the bowl sides and crept onto the yellow-and-blue-painted locker-room floor. The line of unflushed water trickled from the stall to the Mighty Hornets' Nest emblem.

Fat Angie flailed, trying to extract her foot. By the time she opened the stall door, she had a rapt audience. At this pivotal moment, with her clothes dripping from her hand, a flood of thoughts threatened to crack the dam of Fat Angie's "ums."

It was a weak threat, however.

"Um . . ." Fat Angie said, tugging at her water-spotted gym shorts.

The girls laughed.

"What a freak," said one girl.

"And I give you William Anders High's Official Wacko Lesbo, Fat Angie," said Stacy Ann. "Hand-washing your clothes now?"

Fat Angie stuffed her clothes into her backpack. Her soaked sneaker squeaked against the floor and squished her sock between her toes.

"Forget what I said earlier," said a girl. "She'll never make the team."

Fat Angie shoulder-slammed the locker-room door, stumbled up the stairs, and tossed her damp backpack in the stands. She marched onto the court, put her toe to the sideline, and ran lines. Back and forth she ran. Coach Laden emerged from her office and saw Fat Angie burning up the court — well, as much as she could. Her cheeks blazing red.

Her shoes squeaking, slipping. Nothing stopped her. Full-court lines. Then she grabbed a ball off the caddie. She bounced it three times and jammed down the court. Her eyes focused on the target. Fat Angie hit the top of the key. What should have been a dramatic moment, like in a coming-of-age sports film, fell short. She slipped and fell back. The ball rolled away.

Coach Laden had two feet on the court when Fat Angie smacked her palms against the floor and scrambled to her feet. She picked up the ball and zeroed in on the opposite end of the court. She bounced the ball with furiously focused intensity.

Girls began to emerge from the locker room. Stacy Ann leaned in to one of them and said, "I'm shutting this down, now." She stepped onto center court. Stacy Ann lowered her hips into guard position and waited for the robust, pee-smelling Fat Angie to make her move.

Fat Angie ripped down the court. Stacy Ann's steel look should have psyched out the fat girl. But Fat Angie kept her eyes on the target, and when Stacy Ann inevitably came between her and the basketball hoop, Fat Angie, huffing of course, pressed against Stacy Ann.

"Give it up, freak," Stacy Ann said, sliding and shifting with the determined Fat Angie.

Fat Angie backed up. Stacy Ann straightened her defensive stance, indicating that Fat Angie was not a threat.

That was a mistake.

Full of rage, Fat Angie raced for the basket.

Stacy Ann slid her long legs sideways and locked herself into position. Fat Angie let out a primitive scream as she stopped and jump-shot over Stacy Ann's extended arms.

The ball smacked the backboard and toilet-bowled before dropping in. Stacy Ann had been outshot by the Wacko Fatso Dyke formerly known only as Fat Angie.

Fat Angie leaned on her knees and caught her breath.

Coach Laden blew her whistle. All the other girls jogged onto the court. Stacy Ann glared as she walked past Fat Angie. The ball that had sealed the deal rolled to the edge of the court, where KC stood holding her phone in snapshot mode.

"Let's go, Angie," said Coach Laden.

The moment — time — froze between the girls. Fat Angie and KC exchanged super-dramatic-longing looks. KC's was laced with a harder, you-really-betrayed-me-so-I'm-not-revealing-my-heart look. At least, that was what Fat Angie chose to believe about their exchange.

KC pocketed her cell and disappeared around the corner.

Fat Angie dropped her head back, exhaled heavy breaths, and moved in with the rest of the girls.

"Just a reminder, ladies," said Coach Laden. "Varsity has two spots and the next hour and a half determines who walks out with them."

Fat Angie salivated at the yellow-and-blue jerseys with gentle white trim dangling from Coach Laden's hand. She was perplexed by such a reaction without an association to food.

"OK. Let's warm up." Coach Laden blew her whistle and the clock started.

Coach Laden pushed the girls from drill to drill, testing agility, endurance, and hunger.

Fat Angie repeated in her headache-wracked brain, "Don't quit. Don't ever quit."

Her sister had said, *"Remember, you have to follow through. No matter what Mom or anyone says. The only thing in your way is you. And me. Ha!"*

"More, Angie. Let's go," said Coach Laden, startling her.

And so Fat Angie did—go. Again, and again. Her muscles ached. Her legs shook when she did crosscourt defensive slides, but she pushed onward. Imagining her sister cheering her on.

Stacy Ann unleashed the b-ball beast inside her. Her defense was impeccable.

Fat Angie outshot every girl on the court but Stacy Ann.

Coach Laden blew the whistle and the girls limped forward, barely standing. Two jerseys hung over Coach Laden's broad shoulders.

"Who thinks she is the best player out here?" asked Coach Laden.

Fat Angie felt no need to chime in on that question.

Two girls in the front raised their hands confidently. They had played quite well. Very well, as a matter of fact.

"You two can leave," said Coach Laden.

Confused, the girls held their footing.

"Seriously. Leave the court. You're not team players."

One of the girls, clearly a box-dyed blond, said, "Come on, Stacy Ann."

Stacy Ann was not one to follow the sheep.

"Stacy Ann?" said Coach Laden.

"I'll catch you later," Stacy Ann said to the girl.

"Chicken shit," said one of them, as the two left the court.

"Who out here thinks they would be great for JV this year?" said Coach Laden.

A group of hands went up. That group did not include Stacy Ann or Fat Angie. Actually, Fat Angie very much wanted to throw her hand up, but her sister would not have. Her sister would not have quit.

"You two think you're varsity material?" Coach Laden asked, addressing Stacy Ann and Fat Angie.

"I can play hard," said Stacy Ann.

Coach Laden's attention veered to Fat Angie, who had her head unconfidently down. "Angie?"

"Um . . ." Fat Angie said. "I can . . ."

This was her moment. Everything she had been working for came down to whatever she would say next.

Stacy Ann half-laughed.

The tension swelled in Fat Angie's head. The process of counting numbers as a coping device in no way felt accessible.

"I can . . ." said Fat Angie.

They were all waiting. Fat Angie was waiting. She closed her eyes, and in that quiet she could hear her sister's voice.

"I can follow through," Fat Angie said, almost surprised the words were coming out of her mouth. "I won't quit."

There they were. Stacy Ann and Fat Angie. Mortal enemies vying for a chance to play on the state-ranked team to beat.

"That's good," said Coach Laden, handing Fat Angie a jersey. "Don't ever quit."

Fat Angie stretched out her sweaty hand. A varsity jersey — a varsity jersey, freshman year! A varsity jersey freshman year like her sister. She was like her sister! She pressed the yellow-and-blue fabric against her chest. Then —

"Yes! Yes! Yes!" And Fat Angie did a little jump-in-place happy dance.

Stacy Ann and the rest of the hopefuls stared at Coach Laden.

"Um . . ." said Fat Angie, feeling the awkwardness in her behavior. *"Yesss."*

Coach Laden held out the other jersey for Stacy Ann and said, "You play on this team *like* you're on a team or I'll bench you all season."

Stacy Ann nodded.

"The rest of you are JV," said Coach Laden. "Meet with Coach Grates in his office. Good job, everyone."

The girls peeled off for the locker room. Stacy Ann glared at Fat Angie. "This doesn't change anything, Fatso. You'll bench it all season."

"You know what you are?" said Fat Angie.

"Please, Fat Angie. Tell me. What am I?"

Fat Angie's face constricted as she pondered the question. She was not exactly sure but it was extremely unpleasant. That much was a fact.

"You're a freak," said Stacy Ann, resuming her strut for the locker room.

Fat Angie stood there. The court was empty.

She held out the jersey and gulped.

Forty-two. The number on the jersey was forty-two.

It was her sister's number. It was her sister's jersey. Fat Angie poked her arms and head through and stood there awaiting some magical transformation.

She was, of course, still Fat Angie. Fat Angie in a state-winning final-basket-at-the-buzzer jersey. And that had currency.

Re-creating the winning state play, Fat Angie air-dribbled. Her eyes imagined defenders. She passed right, set a screen, pivoted, and pulled out—way out. The ball whipped back to her. She dribbled, whipped it left, eyed the clock, then — right hand in the air. The ball met her palm. Full stop. Straight up, and everything fell away — the defenders, the crowd.

Release.

Buzzer!

Whoosh!

"Forty-two," the crowd had chanted. Over and over, her sister's number had filled the gymnasium.

Right then, there was no crowd. There was no state final. There was Fat Angie. Fat Angie in her sister's jersey, which fit surprisingly better than she could have imagined.

Fat Angie was number forty-two now.

Chapter FOURTEEN

Fat Angie hunched over her sushi takeout. Every ounce of joy regarding her spot on the William Anders High School varsity squad was squashed by an obligatory dinner at the dining-room table with her couldn't-be-bothered mother and Wang.

Fat Angie squeezed the cloth napkin in her lap into a wrinkled ugly thing.

Wang leaned back in his chair and smeared wasabi across his plate.

Her mother poured a second glass of wine. An unusually large glass.

The moment sucked the absolute life out of Fat Angie. She wanted to scream but knew it would be perceived as acting out.

"Eat your sushi," said her mother.

Fat Angie did not like uncooked fish.

Fat Angie did not like uncooked anything that should have been cooked.

Fat Angie did like the noodles but her mother had portion-controlled her carbs to three-fourths of a cup.

Wang sat forward, swirling noodles on his fork. He looked up for only a moment at his sullen sister, who was still wearing the smelly HORNETS' NEST T-shirt.

"I, um . . ." said Fat Angie. "I made the varsity team today."

Fat Angie clung to the jersey from beneath the table. Awaiting some reaction from her mother, who sipped her wine.

"Mom . . ." Fat Angie said.

"Did you call your therapist today?"

"I made the varsity basketball team," Fat Angie said. "I sent you a text."

"I'm not cold, Angie," said her mother. "I know you think I am. I'm not particularly proud of how I handled last night. That's not the point."

"What's the point then?" Wang said, deadpan. He shook his head and slipped iBuds into his ears.

Fat Angie held up the jersey. It was a showstopper of a moment. That jersey had not been in their house since the day after the state finals. Wang fixed his eyes on the jersey. There seemed to have been the slightest break in Connie's otherwise disconnected behavior. Fat Angie's lips formed a smile that puffed up to beautiful cheeks.

"I made the team," Angie repeated. "I did it."

"Return it tomorrow," her mother said.

"What?"

Her mother reached for her cell. "You got that out of pity. You need to learn to live in reality."

"Why are you—can't you just—this *is* reality. I really mean I made it on my own," Fat Angie said.

Her mother tapped the number two on her phone. Otherwise known as speed dial to Fat Angie's therapist.

"I'm not going to let you manipulate me," her mother said.

"How am I—"

"Hello, I need to speak to Dr. Conrad," Connie said. "Well, then I need to leave a message for him. Yes, it is an emergency. Do people generally call after hours to discuss the mundane?"

"You don't share things with my mother," Angie had said to the therapist. *"She can't really be bothered with the truth."*

"Have you tried to communicate with her?"

"I don't have unlimited text messaging."

The therapist had made a note: *Issues of abandonment from father's stroke.*

Her mother hung up the phone. "Your therapist is going to call back on your cell, and when he does, don't you eat through my money with your 'ums.'"

Fat Angie studied her mother splitting a piece of

yellowtail with a few aggressive chopstick maneuvers. "I'm so tired of this, Angie. I don't even know who you are."

"Can you cut her a little slack, Mom?" said Wang. "Or does that just crush your schedule?"

"So the two of you are now joined by disliking me?"

"You just want us to sit here and accept you not being around and Dad not being around and act like we're . . . a fucking Rockwell picture or something," Wang said. "Whatev. That's jank."

Fat Angie watched the standoff between her mother and Wang intensify with an exchange of looks.

"I brought you to this country to give you a better life and—"

"You mean *Dad* brought me here. Then *you* wouldn't let me go with him because you're petty."

Their mother heaved a heavy breath and raised her glass of wine to him. "You're baiting me. You're acting out. Your therapist has made that much clear."

"I bet he has," Wang said, under his breath.

"Excuse me?" said his mother.

Wang kicked back from the table. "You decide to stop being petty, I'll gladly pack out. Until then, don't act like we're so stupid. Angie and I know you're banging my therapist."

"Sit down!" said his mother, shooting out of her seat.

He shook his head, his expression engaged in a serious smirk. "*You* sit down," Wang said.

He jetted upstairs. The grinding of death-metal guitars blasted from his stereo.

"Why?" asked her mother. "Why. Can't. Both of you. Just. *Try,* Angie?"

"Try what?" asked Fat Angie.

"To accept reality," said her mother. "To *be* in reality."

"You mean *your* reality," Fat Angie said, glaring.

"Don't ever feel the freedom to look at me like that, Angie."

Fat Angie closed her eyes and silently counted in her head. Unaware that the numbers began to rip from her chapped lips. Chant-like.

"The numbers will calm you," the therapist had said. *"You will feel—"*

The slap of her mother's hand on the table startled Fat Angie. The wine spilled, rolling to the table edge, drip-smacking on the cream carpet. It would most definitely leave a stain.

"Damn it!" her mother said, sopping up the spill with her overpriced off-white napkin.

Her mother looked so much smaller on the floor, where she feverishly pressed the wounded carpet. The napkin did its best to minimize the injury.

"What?" her mother said.

"Nothing."

"Then quit staring like you've never seen someone clean up a mess. Why do you have to act so incredibly *special*?"

A speedball of anger shot from head to heel. Angie broke for the stairs. She passed Wang's obnoxiously loud music and went into her room. She dug into her backpack and pulled out the crumpled picture of her and KC Romance deep in smoochfest. She cut out the picture and forced it to fit within the confines of the plastic photo holder in her Velcro wallet. She dropped her head forward. The stretch of her neck felt great.

Her cell phone beeped. She flipped it open.

Mom's such a bitch. Wang had attached his signature skull and crossbones to the message.

She sighed.

She started to text back.

She stopped. She could not trust Wang even though he had just called their mother out. He had all the traits and history of a turncoat.

Fat Angie jammed into a pair of jeans that did not fit quite as tightly as she would have expected and crawled out her bedroom window. With shaky muscles, she worked her way down the tree. Just above the dining-room window her sneaker slipped. Her heart revved into turbo pump. She pressed against the tree for absolute dear life. In spite of her being less than eight feet from the ground. Steadying herself, she watched her mother power through documents. The dining room emanated that gold glow common in cheesy made-for-TV Christmas movies. Fat Angie waited for some sign of the person who once was her mother. Not the angry kamikaze pilot-pod person who had taken over her mother when her sister had joined the armed forces.

Fat Angie tapped on KC's bedroom window. The crisp chill crawled up her back and numbed her ears. She blew onto her hands and wished common sense would have had her wear, at the very least, a hoodie.

"KC?" Fat Angie knocked harder.

The neighbor's dog raged at Fat Angie. The entire neighborhood of dogs went into a domino effect of howling, barking.

KC stood at the window, her arms crossed.

"I have to talk to you," Fat Angie said, a gust of wind sending a shiver down her body.

"I'm busy."

"Busy how?" said Fat Angie.

"Just busy."

"I'll be quiet," said Fat Angie.

KC opened the rather sticky window. "You said you had to talk to me, right?"

Fat Angie nodded.

"How are you going to do that and be quiet?"

Conundrum. Fat Angie was in a clear, unexpected conundrum. She thought for a moment.

"I'll show you," said Fat Angie.

"Whatever," KC said, plopping belly-first onto her bed.

Fat Angie struggled and flopped to KC's hardwood

floor. KC flipped through a textbook and jotted down homework in a binder. "You know, somebody might have taken a picture of you coming around the side of the house."

Fat Angie dropped her head. This was not how she had imagined the conversation going.

"Or is that why you didn't use the front door?" KC said. "To avoid the paparazzi?"

"No," Fat Angie said. "I wanted to tell you . . . I made the basketball team. Varsity. My sister and me are the only ones to ever do that as freshmen."

"Well, you'll rise to high ranks of popularity and keggers with the cool kids now," KC said. "Many congrats. You and Jake can be b-ball platonic sweethearts."

"I thought you'd want me to make the team."

"I thought you thought," KC said. "But apparently I was cruising in the mistake lane just like you."

Fat Angie sighed. It was the only response she could act on, though screaming was an option she had not completely ruled out.

"Look, this is getting stale," said KC.

Fat Angie did not follow the trajectory of KC's statement.

"We keep doing this thing," KC said.

"What thing?"

"The kinda tragic breakup-reconciliation thing. You freak out. Then yo-yo back. Recycle. Again and again. It's too teen-romantic-dramedy for me."

Fat Angie, unfamiliar with the genre, was at a loss. Though she understood the underlying meaning. Sort of.

"It's different for you," said Fat Angie. "I'm . . . I like being with you. It's just—"

"Yeah, that's classic." KC sat up and sipped a bottle of organic root beer. "Back in Beverly . . ." KC pulled the framed photo of her and Ms. Pom-Pom from a box beside her bed. "She liked to be with me too. When no one was looking. And if someone thought we might be a little too close, she'd just date another jockazoid. Then crawl through my window at night. Feed me some rich spiel with super-size lies on the side."

"I don't . . ." Fat Angie struggled. "I don't date jocka-zoids. I don't *date.* I don't—I don't know. I mean—"

"What?" said KC, throwing the picture frame on the bed. "Say it, Angie."

"I . . ."

KC stood in front of her. "Say what you wanna say. Can you? Can you be the *you* that likes me inside of my room or behind some poorly kempt shrub?"

Fat Angie swallowed, her face contorting. She fought against her instinct to "um."

"I don't mean all PDA massive," said KC. "But acting like you know me might go a few miles."

"I . . . got scared," Fat Angie said. "Seeing the picture on my locker. Wanting to make the team. I just . . . I'm not cool. I . . . I'm not pretty."

"Yeah, I remember the self-deprecating speech," said KC. "Was kinda standing in your direct line of fire today at lunch. Angie, I'm a cutter in recovery. You think people don't hush-hush trash-talk about me?"

"The whole world hates me," said Fat Angie. "Don't you get it? They hate me. Me. Fat Angie."

"Then hate 'em back. Besides, who needs the whole world?" said KC. "I mean, only a few parts of it are kinda important. And if they all hate someone named Fat Angie, then that's not you. You're Angie."

And right then, the thinner-but-not-slim Angie melted inside.

"Can't you see it? The ultra beautiful and sweet . . . goobtastic Angie. The person who laughs at my panda jokes."

Fat Angie laughed.

"See? And they're really lame jokes," KC said.

In what should have been a tension breaker, Fat Angie took note of KC's arms exposed by a short-sleeved fitted T-shirt. It was the first time she had seen the full extent of KC's scars. They climbed up and down her forearms—stretched to her shoulders. Staring was inevitable for some-one like Angie. Shame was probable for a girl like KC. No matter how beautiful KC looked on the outside.

KC self-consciously jammed herself into a black punk-band hoodie. Ironically, the word SCAB was stitched into the hoodie's breast.

Angie sat beside KC on the bed.

"I told you I'm over it," said KC, sipping the longneck bottle of organic root beer.

"OK," said Fat Angie.

"I mean, Johnny Depp had the same thing. The cutting thing."

"OK," Angie said again.

They sat on the edge of the bed and were wrapped in silence for approximately 12.3 seconds.

"I like your hoodie," Fat Angie said.

"Thanks," KC said.

"It's a really cool kind of black."

Pause.

HUGE PAUSE.

Something had to stop the pause. Then Angie remembered. "I got something for you." She reached into her pocket and pulled out a—

"A Japanese-imported light-up candy ring!" said KC. "Where did you find it?"

"The Five 'N' Go," said Angie. "I stopped by on the way thinking you'd maybe like it."

"I thought they banned them from the U.S.," said KC. "Kids were eating the batteries or something."

"It's Dryfalls, Ohio. It's sorta like living in a different country. As you probably noticed. Look, unwrap here. See. You pull—"

"Here?" asked KC.

"Yeah. And it lights up. For something like two hours."

KC pulled the tab to the Japanese-imported light-up candy ring and read aloud, "'Warning! Not for children under four years of age.' Guess we're cool then."

KC placed the blinking red ring in her mouth. Her cheek flashed like a turn signal.

They sat wrapped in that stifling silence for another 12.3 seconds, give or take a few.

"I was way gay-girl gay before I met you," KC said, her words jumbled by the candy blinking in her mouth.

"Oh. Yeah. Me, too," said Angie.

KC seemed unconvinced by Angie's statement.

"I must've been," Angie said. "I just didn't . . . know."

KC pulled the candy out of her mouth. "The whole freaky arm scar thing. Slice and dice? Started, like, way back in the day. Back when my dad and Esther split ways."

"Sure," said Angie. She had no idea why she said it.

"It's just that . . . sometimes things get really . . . complicated. Really loud. I just want it to be quiet. Sounds crazy, huh?"

"I'm kinda the authority on crazy around here and it doesn't so much sound . . . crazy."

"Yeah. But it's all over now," said KC. "I mean. You know, the slice and dice."

"Did it hurt?" said Fat Angie.

"Of course it hurt," said KC. "Sorta. It's complicated."

"Oh, well, sure it is. I mean, you've said it is."

Pause.

Another pause!

"So your dad . . . ?" asked Angie.

"Complete wedge about the cutting thing . . . the everything. He's been MIA for over a year. He's always got a solid on the excuse. Working late. Working weekends. He's an MD at one of those urgent-care doc-in-the-box places. It's pretty lame."

"Yeah, I haven't really seen my dad much either," said Angie. "He's kinda moved forward in a backward way."

"Yeah?"

"Yeah," Angie said.

"Yeah," said KC. "You know, I guess I'm lucky. Esther would love me even if I were a Martian. You know, with twelve tentacles sprouting from my head and eyeballs in my palms."

Angie knew her couldn't-be-bothered mother would find such appearances unacceptable and seek out whatever medical procedures were available to make her daughter *normal.*

"My mom said I can't talk to you ever again," Angie said.

KC considered this statement with the light-up candy ring blinking once again in her mouth. She removed it quickly and took a deep breath.

"Do you like me?" said KC on the exhale.

The answer seemed so obvious, how could it be anything but a rhetorical question?

"You don't have to answer that," KC said, getting up from the bed. "I'm . . . I push. I don't let people *evolve* into their answers. That's what my last therapist said."

"Therapy sucks," Angie said.

"I don't know. I thought it was pretty cool."

"Mine always says everything backward," Angie said. "Like I'm saying green and he repeats red. But sometimes it's green."

"Sometimes it's red," KC said, watching the candy ring blink on her finger.

Angie zeroed in on the blinking candy ring.

The sheriff's lights had sprayed against the faces of people from the pep rally. So many watching, waiting for something else to happen as they loaded Fat Angie into the back of the ambulance.

"Hey," KC said. "You know what? I'm sick of giving my dad a Get Out of Jail Free card."

What did the game of Monopoly have to do with KC's father? That was when Angie clued in that she was being far too literal.

"See, Angie, I keep lying—pretending I'm someone else with him. Like when he is all Go Fish about my life I say, 'Yeah, I'm dating—a guy!' And I'm not." KC sat on the bed again. "I mean, I'm not all gay pride rah-rah paint-me-like-a-rainbow. But I like . . ."

This juncture confused Angie tremendously. Plus she suddenly felt the very warm urge to pee but felt it wasn't the best time to leave the room. Even if KC did have a private bathroom.

"I wanna tell him," KC said.

"Yeah," Fat Angie said. "Who?"

"My dad," said KC.

"He doesn't know you're gay-girl gay?"

"No way. My dad?" KC said. "I hinted at it once and he blew an entire fuse box. He's super down with the religion since he remarried."

"Then maybe it's not a good idea."

"I'm his daughter," KC said. "He has to love me. It's in the rule book in the 'Don't Be a Jerk' chapter."

KC grabbed her cell from beneath the pillow and hit speed-dial number nine.

"Wait," said Angie. "Maybe . . . maybe you should . . ."

KC's attention hung in the balance of the mighty *should*.

"It's ringing," said KC. "What am I gonna say?"

Angie picked at a thread in KC's purple heart pillow.

"Voice mail," KC said. "Figures."

"KC," said Angie.

"Hey, Dad. It's KC. That's stupid. You know it's me. I'm your daughter. Your *only* daughter, I might add. Unless you dropped seeds that I know absolutely nothing about. OK, that's gonna annoy you. Look, it's cool that you canceled the trip out here this month but I really . . . listen. I'm not being trendy or influenced by Esther, who left you *not* because she's a feminist lesbian but because she thinks you're manipulative and controlling. But that's between the two of you." KC paused. "Anyway, I need to tell you something. And it's really important to me, Dad. Please call me back. I need to tell you —"

His voice mail beeped through her phone. KC dropped her head on the bed. "Voice mail cut me off. I finally have the courage to cards . . . lay them out on the table and I get a disconnect."

"There's a bright side," said Angie.

"What?" asked KC.

"I don't really know. I just kinda said it. It's . . . stupid."

KC sat beside Angie. "No, it's not. Thanks for my ring."

"Sure. I mean, yeah."

"Wow!" KC said, flying back on her bed.

Angie was startled by KC's exclamation.

"I did it," said KC. "Can you believe it? I mean, he won't get the message for a decade because he's a major loser with voice mail but . . . I *said* it. Well, kind of. I'm gonna say it, Angie! I'm gonna say, 'Dad, I'm totally into girls.' No, that's weird. 'Dad, I'm gay.' Huh."

"That's swell," said Angie.

"You think?"

KC reached out and touched Angie's quickly blushing cheek. Her candy ring flashed on and off. "You get this brave thing going on for me."

"Me?"

"Yeah, you," said KC. "I'm not some superhero girl. I mean, that would be way cool. But it's not who I am."

Angie gulped. "You are to me. In a human sorta kinda way. Without a cape."

KC leaned forward, in kissing distance, and that was all Angie could think of. Kissing KC Romance. That and her need to go to the bathroom.

"Um . . ."

"Yeah?" said KC, her root-beer breath breathing onto Fat Angie's lips.

"Capes are stupid," Fat Angie said.

And just like that, their lips met . . . longer than they had during that first session of smooches. This was officially their first kiss. It had fireworks and lightning. It had . . . romance!

Most of all, it didn't have Wang's camera phone lurking in the distance.

Chapter FIFTEEN

In a week of young-love bliss accompanied by a heavy helping of social ostracism, the unbelievable reality that Fat Angie was the second freshman to make the varsity championship basketball team went as viral as Wang's cell-phone photograph.

Kids huddled between bells and secretly tapped text messages:

Can u believe?

Can U?

But she's so fat . . .

Not as fat . . .

At the height of the gossip frenzy, it was rumored that she had shot up performance-enhancing drugs, as there could be no other explanation for her sudden athletic prowess. Fat Angie was now under the microscope not for her vast pants size, but for how she continued to almost magically perform on the basketball court practice after practice. The buzz was red-hot!

Fat Angie no longer rode the bus with the heckling Duo of Geekdom. Basketball practice started every day at exactly 3:10 p.m. Drill after drill. At times it all began to blur for Fat Angie, but she fought the blur. She fought the dry mouth and pains in her diaphragm. And while speed and agility were not her strong suits, when the ball touched her fingers, she was almost unstoppable at the basket. With every release, she let out the slightest whisper from her lips . . . like a prayer. Not a wish for the ball to find its way through the hoop. A wish that her sister would come home, throw her arms around Angie, and say, "I'm proud of you," or something all Hallmark special-esque. She just had to not quit!

Stacy Ann focused less on her Fat Angie attack campaign and more on Coach Laden's developing her into the kind of point guard who stood out. Reason being that Stacy Ann came from a family of four overly successful siblings and overcompensated for her fear of failure.

"She's overcompensating," KC said, strutting into her bedroom with two steaming plates of whole-wheat fettuccine.

Angie followed with a couple cans of Sprite.

"Even so, Stacy Ann is *amazing* at point," Angie said.

"Talent for the defense, I'll grant you, but super flawed as an earthling."

The girls plopped on floor pillows, KC clicking the remote.

"*Buffy* marathon on Syfy," said KC. "Absolute. While not as retro as some of your faves — excluding *Freaks and Geeks,* which is ultra-even — I think this will be a *W* in the win column."

Angie twirled her pasta on a spoon.

"Hey," KC said, with fettuccine hanging from her lips. "Why the sad face?"

Angie shrugged. "I . . . miss her."

"I know."

"Sometimes. It's like . . . I'm still there. In the kitchen, hearing about her missing. But then there's this other . . . clawing guilt if a couple hours pass and I haven't thought about her."

"Maybe you can miss her and not have to hurt every second," KC said.

Angie picked at a hole in her sneaker. She nodded with a repetition more to soothe herself than to agree with KC.

"Tomorrow," Angie said. "I get to wear her jersey and be on the court and —"

Angie's cell phone played Beethoven's Fifth Symphony.

"My mom," Angie said, clicking it to voice mail.

"Sweet ringtone," said KC. "That would crack Esther into pieces if I did that to her."

Angie listened to the message.

"What's the verdict?" KC asked.

"She's back from New York," Angie said.

"Thought she was gonna be gone longer," KC said.

"Yeah, me too. Anyway, she wants me home for a fake family meal."

"It's crystal," KC said, softly squeezing Angie's hand. "I'll see you tomorrow. And if it goes south, I'm here."

There was a simultaneous lean in. The kiss was effortlessly intense. The warm plates resting on their legs clanked. KC's hand pressed against Angie's face. Angie's hand squeezed KC's waist. The kiss kicked some most definite ass.

KC pulled back, their heads touching. "You better—"

"Yeah . . . I better," Fat Angie said. "But . . ."

The girls locked lips once more with the *Buffy the Vampire Slayer* theme song playing in the background. It was not the most romantic music but would most definitely do.

Fat Angie hunched over her dinner. It was the first family dinner since the Slap That Spilled the Sake, as Fat Angie had written in her letter to her sister. Shifting in his seat, Wang picked at a zit with one hand and speed-texted with the other. His earbuds seeped goth metal. Fat Angie knew for a fact that Wang did not like goth metal and was playing the music to irritate their overly perfumed mother.

"You look thinner," said her mother, not looking away from her BlackBerry.

"I guess," said Fat Angie. "How was New York?"

Scrolling through her e-mail, her mother said, "Unusually cold."

"Yeah?" asked Angie.

"Don't eat too many noodles," her mother said. "Here. Try the soup."

"I don't like soup."

"Everyone likes soup," said her mother. "I met a Belgian man in New York. He eats soup before every dinner. Every one."

"I'm not Belgian," said Fat Angie.

Her mother sighed. "That isn't the point, Angie."

Her mother positioned the soup container in front of Wang, who acknowledged it with the slightest raise of his eyes before tapping on his iPod.

Fat Angie's mother poured a second glass of red wine, which would have been inconsequential if she had not mentioned drinking two glasses already on the plane from New York.

"How hard is it to leave out the things you don't ask for?" asked her mother, tucking snow peas in the crevices between her plate and charger. "I order the same thing every time."

"Mom," Fat Angie said.

"What?"

"My first game's tomorrow."

"What game?" asked her mother, distracted by an incoming text.

"Varsity basketball," said Fat Angie.

Her mother nodded. "Right. And you'll be starting? Featured player?"

"I probably won't play, no," said Fat Angie. "Just thought if you were in town you might want to come or something."

"Did you go to therapy on Tuesday?"

Fat Angie sensed a trap.

"Didn't think so," said her mother, picking up her plate with cell phone in tow.

Connie dispensed of the healthy takeout, slipped the plate in the dishwasher, and left the room.

Wang, who seemed engrossed in his loud music and texting, directed his attention toward his sister. "Hey."

"Turncoat," she said, getting up from the table.

"Huh?"

Fat Angie scowled at him and, racing upstairs, tugged at her shorts leg creeping up her thigh.

She was halfway out her bedroom window when Wang knocked. Fat Angie smacked her head against the windowsill.

"Do we no longer have a front door?" he said.

Rubbing her head, Fat Angie crawled back in. "Thanks to you I have to crawl out windows to avoid Mom."

"Sorry about that," he said.

"Like you care. What do you want?"

"You seem to be doing all right. The basketball thing," he said.

"Why, do you wanna ruin that too?" she asked.

"I said I was sorry."

"I said I hate you," Fat Angie countered.

"Yeah." He flipped the brim of his hat around.

"So?" she asked.

He picked at a fleck of paint on the doorway.

"I could come to your game tomorrow," Wang said sheepishly, stepping into the room.

She half-laughed. "Why? So you can take a picture of me bent over and explode the size of my butt on the Internet?"

"Look, OK. I know I've kinda been a douche cake to you."

"I don't even know what that is," Angie said. "But if it's like being a jerkface, then yeah, you have. How could you do that, Wang? You're my brother. I mean, why?"

"Shit, I don't know," Wang said. "It just sorta happened. It seemed like it would be funny. But then it wasn't. And I'd already sent it to, like, ten people. Then it was, like, boom-gone everywhere."

Angie stood with her arms crossed, not giving him an inch.

"So . . . I have a picture of Stacy Ann without a bra," Wang said.

"Do not."

"Do," he fired back.

"Do not."

"Do to infinity and beyond," he said, a twinge of superiority in his voice.

"Do not to infinity and beyond times pi," said Angie.

The ultimate bluff-calling challenge had been made.

He slid his phone out of his back pocket. In three quick clicks, there was Stacy Ann without a bra. "A chick in your gym class sold it to me. It wasn't cheap."

"That's gross," Fat Angie said.

"You're into girls."

"But not Stacy Ann. And not all pervy-photo-without-permission."

He clicked the keypad. "I thought you'd think it was fresh."

Fat Angie, being Wang's recent archenemy, found this pseudoreconciliation perplexing.

"I guess it's kinda cool. But still pervy," she said. "Get a hobby that doesn't involve nudie pics."

"So I should try out for the basketball team and act like my dead sister?"

"She's not dead," Fat Angie said. "Take it back, Wang." She punched his shoulder. "Take it back."

"OK, recanted," he said. "But Mom's gonna lock you up again if you don't snap back into goody-goody sane. And you can take that to the bank. The—"

"The blood bank. I know. Stop quoting that stupid Steven Seagal film. He's not a good role model anyway."

"Better than *Growing Pains,*" he said.

"It's a perfectly good family show."

"If you live in a glass house and grew up in the 80s, maybe. Touch down on planet Earth and watch some MTV."

"They don't even play music videos."

"Who cares?" He tapped a text. "It will at least make you feel like everyone else."

"We were never like everyone else."

Pause.

"You gonna split?" he asked.

Fat Angie dropped back on her bed. "Maybe not."

Wang sat down beside her. She wiggled, creating an additional foot and a half to equal two and a half feet between them. Her bed was only five feet in length and she slept in the fetal position to maintain all body parts on the mattress.

Wang speed-tapped another text. "She sent a text."

"What?" Angie sat up.

"It was a couple of days before she was taken. I didn't tell anybody."

"What did it say?"

"Stuff, you know," Wang said.

"Don't be a jerk. Wang . . ."

He clicked through his phone and showed Angie a locked message. It was a photo of her sister and a puppy in

Iraq. She was decked in her camo gear and smiling with all the light that was her. The message read, "Miss U."

"Why didn't you ever show me this?" Angie asked.

Wang got up off the bed. "I wanted something to be mine, I guess. After she went missing, I dunno. That's all I had. I knew she wasn't coming back."

"You don't know that. She never quits."

"That's what pisses me off about you," he said. "Why can't you see what's really happened? Yo, I have. Instead you stuff your face or go shooting hoops like you're her—"

"So I should just thug it? All baggy-blasting clothes, and, um, rap music you hate? Getting into trouble to just check out? You were different before."

"Well, it's not before. Don't you get it? She's not some comic-book hero. She's just like us. She's lost." Wang jammed his cell phone in his jeans. "Maybe they won't find her. Ever."

"I don't believe that," said Fat Angie.

"Yeah, OK," Wang said dismissively. "I gotta jet."

Wang strutted toward the door.

"Wang?"

"Yeah?" he said.

"I really liked it better when you weren't a turncoat."

His smile kicked to one side. Then he left.

Fat Angie's family gave up on her sister when the weeks tallied into months. Her dad could not afford the luxury of a hotel beyond the first ten days. And her mother only let him in the house for an ABC *World News* interview. She did, after all, need everyone to know that the family was intact. Even if the dust on the divorce papers had more than settled.

Angie had told her therapist, *"My mom says, 'We can't let the terrorists think they are ripping us apart.' And I said, 'They* are *ripping us apart.'"*

"How did your mother respond?"

"She told me not to slouch in front of the camera."

The therapist had made a note: *Struggles with interpersonal communication.*

Fat Angie sat in the thick stench of Wang's — of her family's — shared reality. But she would not be swayed. Her sister was going to come home.

Chapter SIXTEEN

Fat Angie had mastered bench warming as the Mighty Hornets' Nest squad pounded through their first three games. But the key to an undefeated season started with beating the state-ranked Tamblyn Titans. The Titans were wicked tall, wicked mean, and just plain wicked young women.

The crowds on both sides of the gymnasium were revved long before the game began and exploded with the game in full throttle.

Jake and KC sat at opposite ends of the bleachers. Both cheered Fat Angie on as she sank every basket during the warm-up. But with the game in play, she was firmly on the bench once again. Two senior players separated her from Stacy Ann, who still refused to give Fat Angie her due for her on-the-court skills. Fat Angie stared, as she was prone to do at times, at her rival. Her rival who was being called in to the game with two minutes left in the first half. Throwing attitude and a slick set of ball-handling skills, Stacy Ann leveraged her team ahead by three at the half.

It was late in the second half when three key Hornets' Nest players had fouled out. Coach Laden looked to the end of the bench, where a minimum of three feet separated Fat Angie from the rest of the squad.

"Substitution," Coach Laden told the supertoned female referee with a tattoo of a four-leaf clover peeking from beneath her zebra-striped polo sleeve. "Number forty-two." Coach Laden looked to Angie, who had zoned out. "Angie, let's hustle."

Fat Angie sprang off the bench and tugged her shorts away from her crotch. Coach Laden held on to her arm and said, "Stick to the fundamentals. Do what you know."

And with a tap on her back, Fat Angie was sent into battle. Stacy Ann, dripping in sweat and red faced, executed her famous glare.

The Hornets' Nest tossed the ball inbounds. Stacy Ann caught and dribbled it, her eyes scanning for an open teammate.

Fat Angie fought to stave off her guard in an elbow-slugging match under the basket. An aggressive six-foot-two Titan who had failed to wear deodorant was all over her.

"Cut it out," Fat Angie said.

"Ref!" shouted Coach Laden about the gorilla girl covering Fat Angie.

Stacy Ann dribbled. The shot clock was running out. No one was open. She had to do something. She had to . . . What happened next would be the talk of Dryfalls for years to come.

Fat Angie pushed away from her defender. She pressed to the front of the key, set a screen on Stacy Ann's guard, and opened up a path for the wretched girl. Stacy Ann drummed for the goal. Fat Angie pivoted and followed the shot that bounced off the rim. With all her might, she leaped, pulled the ball into her, and swung her elbows like an injured snake willing to strike at anything. She shot back up and scored.

Fat Angie scored!

She actually scored in a real game!

The Hornets' Nest crowd shot into the air. The high-school drum corps ripped out a cadence. But the game was one of speed, and the ball was back in play before Fat Angie could bask in her newfound glory.

Fat Angie fought through her exhaustion as she sprinted up and down the court. She fought the overzealous six-foot Titan guarding her like she was on suicide watch. Nothing would stop Fat Angie. If the ball made it to her hands, she would do everything she could to convert the opportunity into two points — or three points! How could it be humanly possible for a wacko fatso newbie-lesbo to display such ability without performance-enhancing drugs? It was not the magic of the jersey that the Hornets' Nest fans had begun to chant. It was not the magic of her sister's HORNETS' NEST T-shirt beneath the jersey. It was simple. Angie felt that her sister was right there, beside her.

The Hornets' Nest team had foolishly expired their time-outs with less than fifteen seconds on the clock. The Titans taunted their opponents with the ball and a one-point lead. Stacy Ann made her best attempt to jostle the ball out of the hands of the Titans' point guard but lost her balance. This left a hole wide enough in the key for the fast lanky girl to drive. The Hornets' Nest team flushed toward the key. Fat Angie pushed away from the girl she was guarding, ran toward the point guard blazing up the key, and stopped. Her feet planted. Her arms went up, and Fat Angie screamed that primitive scream. The Titan point guard shouted back and plowed Fat Angie down.

The supertoned female referee with a tattoo of a four-leaf clover peeking from beneath her zebra-striped polo sleeve blew her whistle. "Foul. Number fifty-four, red. Two."

Foul? This was a scenario Fat Angie had not considered. Sure, there were fantasies of scoring the winning basket, but those were mere fantasies. With one second left on the clock, she had two chances at tipping the scales. Two chances to be all she could be without enlisting in the armed forces. Fate had thrown her a bone and she was completely, absolutely, without a single doubt unsure if she was dog enough to catch it.

Fat Angie rolled onto her knees and struggled up.

"Fatso," said one of the Titan girls, who bumped Fat Angie back down.

"Hey!" yelled Coach Laden at the snarky Titan.

But the referees were too busy making small talk. Perhaps setting up a drink or two after the game. Getting knocked down did not do much for Fat Angie's self-esteem.

A Hornets' Nest teammate helped Fat Angie up. Stacy Ann sneered. "Don't screw it up, Fatty."

"She's on our team, Stacy Ann," said a senior teammate. "Suck it up or sit out."

Stacy Ann stared at Fat Angie as she stepped up to the free-throw line. The referee handed Angie the basketball and moved behind her.

Fat Angie had practiced the free throw to no end. She knew it was the key component to any winning game. Ball handling, layups, three-pointers. These were fundamentals that would take skill, or a substantial amount of time, to harness. The free throw, however, had been her sister's specialty while playing for William Anders High. It was something Fat Angie had studied year after year of her sister's games. And right then it was Fat Angie's specialty, or so she had to quickly convince herself while a gymnasium full of people watched—with KC and Jake looking on from opposite ends of the stands—with the notion that some mythical connection would allow her sister to hear the *whoosh* of nothing but net wherever she was.

No pressure, of course.

The cheerleaders cheered. Coach Laden paced. And Stacy Ann Sloan stood at the key, her eyes searing Fat Angie. Her lips mouthed, "Don't fuck it up, wacko."

Fat Angie's armpits sweated.

Her head sweated.

Even the backs of her knees were slimy.

She wiped her clammy hands on her damp shorts.

"You can sink it, Angie!" Jake's voice pierced the silence.

"Go, Angie!" said KC, in a rhythm of competition with the hunky Jake Fetch.

But could she? That was the question that hovered like an alien spacecraft prepared to abduct her. A bright light suddenly went off in her brain.

She was not her sister. She was Fat Angie.

Her head swung from one side of the gymnasium to the other. Then down the key of annoyed players, waiting for her to botch the shot. Most of them, anyway.

Fat Angie backed away from the free-throw line.

This was, by all rules and regulations associated with the game of basketball, an unusual act. Not an act ever dramatized in sports films. The referees were stumped as Angie jogged off court and toward the concrete stands to KC. KC pushed through the Hornets' Nest crowd and squatted where Fat Angie held on to the red railing.

"I'm scared," said Fat Angie.

"This is it," KC said. "You know, where the sky clears—where something big is right around the corner."

"And you can see a pocketful of stars," Fat Angie said.

"Yeah," KC said. "It all lines up. You feel it, right?"

"Yeah," said Fat Angie. "I think. I mostly wanna throw up."

"Yeah," said KC.

Fat Angie smiled. KC smiled. Ignoring the obnoxious fans and even Coach Laden, KC wrapped her hand around Fat Angie's. Then KC's cell phone rang, jolting them back into reality. Coach Laden fished Fat Angie away. The girls' hands pulled apart.

"Angie, it's just two points," said Coach Laden, reassuring Fat Angie. "Just concentrate."

Fat Angie smiled. "Yeah."

Then something unexpected occurred to Fat Angie. As though the thought had come to her in a spiritual revelation. "I am special," she said, looking at KC, who jammed a thumbs-up while talking on her cell.

Fat Angie looked to Coach Laden.

Coach Laden followed the trajectory of the moment. "Exceptionally special."

Angie jogged back to the free-throw line.

The referee warned Angie about leaving the court. Angie picked up the ball and dribbled it exactly five times. Squinted at the basketball hoop. And with absolutely no hesitation, bent her knees, flicked her wrist, and . . .

Whoosh!

Nothing but net.

The Hornets' Nest crowd went ballistic. She had done it. She had made it. She had tied the game!

Angie's eyes shot to the stands. Jake whipped his fist in the air, and KC—

KC was gone.

The referee handed the ball to Angie.

"You can do it, Angie," Coach Laden shouted from courtside.

Angie's eyes focused only on that rim as she again dribbled five times. Her arms went up and she closed her eyes as it released. In the split moment of release, Angie saw her sister. The two of them shooting hoops on the backboard over the garage. Wang jumping in. The three of them. Together. Not all perfect but—

Swoosh! The Hornets' Nest crowd sprang to their feet!

It was the Disney-esque ending Angie had prayed for. She had won the game. A big game. She had done it!

Only she was not lifted in the air by her teammates as Ralph Macchio had been in 1984's Academy Award–nominated film *The Karate Kid.* They ran right past her to Coach Laden. One girl said in passing, "Way to go, Fat Angie."

As if Fat Angie were in fact her real name.

Nevertheless, the inner beaming of one said game-winning girl could not be squashed. She looked up at that rim and whispered, "Whoosh . . ."

Her sister had to have heard—*felt* the moment when Angie had won the game.

Angie looked into the stands. No KC. Just Jake throwing a nod, then shooting his arms in the air with an explosive *V* for victory.

Stacy Ann clipped Angie's shoulder.

"You're afraid of *everything,*" said Angie. "And I *know* it. And that's why you don't like me."

Stacy Ann shook her head. This gesture, plus her smirk, unbalanced Angie's confidence. "I don't *like* you because you think everyone owes you something because your sister went missing. My dad's been over there twice. He lost three fingers. Do you see CNN at my house? Your whole family soaks up every ounce of light around here, so excuse me for not bowing down to you, your victim-ness."

Stacy Ann disappeared behind the locker-room door.

Angie had not considered that Stacy Ann Sloan's dislike for her could be something other than a one-dimensional mean-girl kind of hate. Stacy Ann had genuine feelings about what was clearly accurate. No one had paid attention to her father in the same way that they had Angie's sister. If they had, Angie had not noticed. Perhaps because she had been preoccupied with her own sadness.

Angie did not know how to translate this epiphany in the letter to her sister. Perhaps she would embellish ever so slightly, so she would not appear to be as insensitive as she suddenly felt.

Chapter SEVENTEEN

During the course of traveling from A to B—A being the away-game town and B being her high school—Angie wrote endlessly. While the team gabbed and laughed, while all of them were marinating in the juices of victory, Angie was elsewhere. She was in Iraq, imagining that by some miracle her sister had in fact wandered out of the desert and found a squadron. They were rushing her to a hospital—clearly she would be dehydrated—and the much-awaited press conference was imminent. Angie's fingers gripped the uni-ball 0.7 roller-ball pen with incredible deliberateness through the whole journey—approximately forty-five minutes, give or take a minute.

She transcribed at length the details of the game. Her fierce struggle to overcome adversity and to become the young woman she was. Similar to what Coach Laden had described to her when she had fought Stacy Ann Sloan in gym class. It felt as though the fight had happened eons ago, but her sister would understand the eons feeling.

Angie paused.

She did not like feeling insensitive about Stacy Ann and had yet to include it in her letter. She twisted around in her seat and peered around the side. Stacy Ann crunched up alone. Eyes closed. Head bobbing from the bumpiness of the ride. Perhaps this would be the time to approach Stacy Ann. To acknowledge her feelings of exclusion. Just as Angie's butt lifted for takeoff, the bus hit a pothole. Stacy Ann's head slammed against the window. Angie braced herself in a midlean hover over Stacy Ann.

"What?" Stacy Ann said.

"Timing is everything," her sister had always said. *"B-ball, people. It's all timing."*

Timing involved math, and Angie remained deficient at the art of numbers.

In short, that moment hovering above Stacy Ann was very bad timing.

"Um. Uh-uh," Angie said, pushing up and away.

She flopped back in her seat.

Angie uncapped her pen and continued her letter. Rather than embellishing, she reconstructed the actual details of her thoughts. Minus the questions of her burnout therapist and her couldn't-be-bothered mother. There. Right then. No detail was too small. Nothing could be left out, because her sister would want to know everything. Good and bad. The way she had always wanted to know everything. Her sister did in fact see Angie fully. When she was simply Angie, as she recently had become to KC.

The bus pulled up to William Anders High. The team charged off with the energy of a hundred victorious warriors. Many of them jammed into the compact energy-efficient cars their parents forced them to drive and kicked up gravel as they sped out of the parking lot.

Angie enclosed the letter to her sister in a six-by-nine envelope. Peeling off a preprinted label with her sister's last known mailing address, she centered it with care. It was absolutely perfect.

"Angie, you all right?" called Coach Laden from the front of the bus.

"Yeah."

"Going to lock you up in here," said Coach Laden.

Angie dragged her tired legs down the aisle.

"Good game," said Coach Laden. "See you Monday."

Angie stepped off the bus. No Wang. Just Jake. Jake without Ryan.

She swung her duffel over her shoulder. " Hey," she said to Jake.

Angie speed-dialed Wang's cell. Voice mail. "Hey, where are you?" she asked.

"That was some shot," Jake said.

"Wasn't too bad, huh?"

"No, you definitely rocked the board." Jake jammed his hands in his hoodie.

"Thanks. I mean, really . . . thanks," Angie said.

Jake nodded.

"So, Wang was supposed to give me a ride," Angie said. "Though I shouldn't be surprised he bailed."

"Yeah, he got hung up," Jake said. "Kicked me a text to give you a lift."

"He's probably engaged in the criminal element, as my mom says."

Jake blew on his hands. "C'mon. I'm freezing."

The ride from the high school toward Oaklawn Ends was a short one, but long enough for Angie to pop off half a dozen texts to KC with no reply.

When they turned into the cul-de-sac of Oaklawn Ends, Angie's couldn't-be-bothered mother stood at the curb of their driveway. She seemed unusually bothered. Angie's pulse elevated. Her palms sweated. Something was . . . off.

"Jake?" said Angie.

He could not look at her.

Angie popped the pimp silver door handle and stepped out. Jake pulled in to his driveway. Ryan blazed through the open back gate.

Ryan was a good dog.

Jake was a good boy.

"What's . . . going on?" said Angie to her mother. She saw Wang in his second-story bedroom window.

He had been crying. He was crying. Wang showed no signs of crying on average and that was a fact that troubled Angie.

"Your dad—"

"Something's wrong with Dad?"

"He's on the way," finished her mother.

"Wh—wh—why?"

Then it happened. The silence.

It took only a moment for Angie to realize. In a film, the camera would have circled around her.

Again and again and again.

Fat Angie dropped her duffel bag and tore the poorly stitched zipper apart.

Her mother, ill equipped for such an outburst, knelt. "What are you doing? Come inside."

Fat Angie ripped into her bag and tossed clothes onto the driveway. She raced to their mailbox with her sister's letter, threw it inside, and lifted the red flag. Her sore hands shook as she gripped the mailbox.

The box was cold.

"Angie," said her mother.

"One, two, three, four, five, six . . ."

"Stop it," said her mother.

Angie looked up to Wang's second-story bedroom window again.

Wang was crying. He was crying a lot.

"Ten, eleven, twelve . . ." The numbers were difficult to form. Her concentration shattered.

Her mother grabbed Angie's shoulders and the sweaty teen twisted, screamed. Her grip on reality had wavered. Angie clawed the envelope out of the mailbox and shouted at her mother, "One, two, three, four, five!"

Angie backed away, seeing Jake and his good dog Ryan sitting on the curb.

Jake was crying.

Ryan sat on his haunches.

Neighbors emerged from their doors. The sounds of news reports seeped from their flat-screen, surround-sound televisions.

Missing

Found

"Angie, stop," her mother said.

It was all so loud. Too loud. Angie squinted at the overcast sky. A helicopter flew overhead. Angie screamed again. And again.

Jake stood.

Ryan stood.

"It's not like we didn't know she wasn't coming back," her mother said, trying to hold her daughter. "Angie, it's OK. You can be OK."

Her mother's voice had quivered only for a moment. It wasn't enough for Angie.

The blades of the helicopter ricocheted in Angie's ears.

Wang was crying. A lot.

Ryan barked at the helicopter as it passed.

Jake moved toward Angie.

"You *can* be OK," pleaded her mother.

Screaming her numbers, Angie sprinted at top speed down the street. Neighbors looked on, barely pretending not to.

"Angie!" shouted her mother.

Angie's counting echoed as she cut out the entrance to Oaklawn Ends. The trucks with satellites . . . the bloggers . . . the photographers . . . they would all return. It would be of interest to the whole world. They would want the skinny—the scoop. The everything.

She ran faster.

Harder.

Her breath was shallow. Her chest hurt.

They would ask their stupid questions. The country would mourn. The president would call, again. What could *he* know? What could *anyone* really know? They were watching. Just watching.

Eighteen minutes and twenty-two seconds later, Angie raced up KC's lawn. She pounded on the door.

"Three hundred and four, three hundred and five . . ."

She pounded on the door harder.

"Three hundred and twelve, three hundred and thirteen . . ."

She stepped over Esther's recently cut-back bush and around the side of the house to KC's bedroom window.

"Three hundred and eighteen, three hundred and nineteen . . ." Angie's knuckles rhythmically drummed the window.

She heard the muted sounds of an undetermined genre of music as she picked up a rock and slammed it through the window. Still counting, fumbling to twist the lock, she cut her arm in several not-so-critical areas. Angie opened the window and flopped in, a piece of glass jamming in her thigh. She did not notice the glass, as her attention was still focused on counting and moving toward the source of the ever-swelling music behind KC's bathroom door.

"Three hundred and—" Angie swung the bathroom door open.

Angie stood still.

The numbers stopped.

Angie's eyes went from a bloody handprint on the floor to KC's beautiful brown eyes, which had seemed to go black. KC kicked the boom box off the tub ledge. The CD skipped before it crashed onto the floor. Electric sparks ignited.

KC's forearms—her beautiful shoulders.

Blood.

Dripping.

Blood.

So many . . . cuts.

"Get out!" KC said.

Angie could not shake off the — the everything. Her shoulders tensed. Her throat tensed.

"Um . . . she . . . um — "

"I don't want you here, *Fat Angie*!"

Angie shivered. The words *Fat Angie* had never, ever leaped from the sweet luscious lips of KC Romance. The grief-stricken Angie could not rationalize the behavior. No set of equations came to mind. She was not prepared for such cruelty.

Angie did not scream.

She did not cry.

She did not even count.

Simply, her fists unclenched. The letter to her sister only whispered as it hit the bathroom floor.

"KC," called Esther. "Your dad's — KC!"

Esther pushed past Angie.

"No baby, no," said Esther.

"Get out, Esther," KC said. "Get out!"

"Not gonna happen, kid." Esther dampened a washcloth. "Angie, honey — "

Sobbing, KC kicked the wastebasket. "I have to cut it out!"

"Shh," Esther said, her voice soothing and safe. "What do you have to get out, baby?"

"He hates me! Dad hates me, Esther," KC said. "He told me he wasn't coming around if I was gonna *play* gay. Play?"

Esther tapped the washcloth against KC's cuts. "He's just a son of a bitch sometimes. I'm sorry, baby."

It was not safe here, Angie thought. Not at KC's.

Angie stepped back from the doorway, her shaky steps disconnected from herself. Glass crackled beneath her sneakers. The sound shredded her ears.

"Angie?" called Esther from the bathroom.

Angie walked at a vigorous pace out of KC's room.

"Hey, Angie," said Mike. "Angie?"

She swung open the front door and burst off the porch. Running. Chafing the inside of her thighs. She felt nothing.

The details as to Angie's whereabouts from A to B were hazy. In this instance, A being KC's home and B being the Five 'N' Go.

The bell dinged above the door as she entered the four-aisle establishment that was under new ownership and being renovated. As if on autopilot, she marched to the Swiss Rolls. She gathered them in her bloody arms and then turned to Sno Balls, M&M's, and whatever assortment of sugary substances caught her eye. Fat Angie approached the counter. A few items dropped from the heaping mountain of junk food.

A skater dude behind the counter gaped at the stockpile of junk food. Clearly he was in the midst of a Mary Jane high, as could be assessed by his glassy eyes.

"Hey," he said. "You know your leg's bleeding."

She looked down. In fact, it was.

"OK, so, you wanna add a Super Slam Soda Slush for eighty-five cents?" he asked.

"No," she said. "Just this."

"It's really good. I had one and you can suicide it with—"

"No!" she said. "Just this."

He sniffed, scratching the top of his greasy head.

"OK, whatever," he said as her eyes filled with hate—with anger—with hunger.

"Nineteen eighty-four," he said.

The number lingered in her head.

She dug into her moist tube sock and flicked a smelly wet twenty at him. She hauled the bag off the counter.

"You want your change?" he asked.

She pushed the door open. The bell dinged.

"Have a nice day," said the skater dude behind the counter.

She stared at him.

"What?" he asked.

She pushed out the door as a car ripped into the parking lot. Music blaring with a garage band hoping to sound like the Smashing Pumpkins song "Bullet with Butterfly Wings":

"Everything's ending
No new beginning

No claim to little fame
There you go waking
In the middle of your hellish reign . . ."

With the Five 'N' Go door still ajar, the punk-Goth-Amish kid in the midst of extreme Rumspringa popped out the driver's side. His engine still running.

"Your leg's, like, bleeding," he said, nonchalant.

She looked down. In fact, it still was.

She nodded.

He shrugged and dipped inside. The music seemed to chase her as she marched on the spit-out-gum-and-stamped-out-cigarette-covered sidewalk to the back of the Five 'N' Go.

"No matter where you turn
You're everything you hate
No matter where you run
You can't be anyone
EMPTY THING . . . !"

She hunkered beside a stack of pallets.

She tore at the Swiss Roll package with her perfectly straight teeth.

As if famished, she jammed the rolls into her plump cheeks. A wave of panic swam from her gut to her heart.

Ripping at package after package, she stuffed one Little Debbie after another into her body. Tears streamed down her face. She sobbed, face full of Little Debbie's sweet Swiss Rolls.

Fat Angie beat her temples with her palms. Harder and harder. Threw her elbows into the concrete store wall. Then leaned forward and upchucked.

It didn't look at all like a Swiss Roll.

Shaking, she curled up on the greasy ground and pulled off her sweatshirt. Her chin doubled as she stared down at the HORNETS' NEST T-shirt.

Her sister would never know of Fat Angie's triumph of good over evil. She would never know about KC Romance. She would never know how utterly lonely Angie's world was without her sister.

These facts were unbearable.

The gusty wind blew Angie's hair straight back. She dragged her feet down Oaklawn Ends' dead-end street. The press was packed in all along the cul-de-sac. Jake and Ryan cut through the crowd and jogged toward Angie.

"Hey," Jake said. "Your leg's bleeding."

She nodded, stoic, and sat on a curb.

Jake sat beside her.

"I don't think your mom meant to hurt you," Jake said.

Angie leaned her head against Jake's shoulder. Expensive cologne emanated from his gray name-brand hoodie.

"My sister's not coming home, Jake," Angie said.

Jake leaned his head on her head and Ryan sat in front of them. As a storm approached, the three of them waited. For whatever was next.

Chapter EIGHTEEN

Fat Angie quietly suffered through her sister's Catholic funeral Mass. She sat in such a way that she seemed to have shriveled, to have dramatically dropped thirty-nine and a half pounds. She had, in fact, not. Not in physical weight anyway.

She walked behind her couldn't-be-bothered mother, who was accompanied by Wang's therapist. Wang kept his iPod on during the wake, the Mass, and the exit from the church. This action did not feel disrespectful in the least to Fat Angie.

Her dad, his shiny wife, and his perfect kids, a boy and a girl of equal height, were also there. Fat Angie's dad reached to hold her hand. She chose to let it brush by her.

Vans of television crews staked out every possible exit and descended on the mourners. Cameras flashed.

Microphones were jammed in the family's faces. The set of ridiculous questions that had befallen them when her sister went missing had been revived in her death.

Fat Angie said nothing.

Coach Laden and the Hornets' Nest basketball team pushed the cameras aside, making a small path to the limousine. A limousine for the family — minus, of course, her sister. Her sister had come home in pieces. Parts. Igniting a maelstrom of opinions about the war. Generating headlines and sound bites. And in the midst of flowers and cards, her couldn't-be-bothered mother was as poised as a grieving politician, granting exclusive interviews to national evening news programs. In the end, Fat Angie's sister's death had become a circus — a sideshow for hundreds of mourners along the edges of the church and anyone with TV or Internet access. It seemed to become everyone's sadness. Except Fat Angie's. She had yet to cry. Not a tear.

Her mother had requested a military burial. Flag on casket and gun salute. The whole nine yards. Fat Angie would have preferred a few yards less. The guns fired. The bugle played. The American flag was folded and extended to the grieving mother, who was in a semi-stoic trance. Fat Angie took note of her mother's behavior but did not save it for later recollection. Rather, she fumed.

In what would be remembered as the onset of Fat Angie's second nervous breakdown, she walked away from her white wooden chair at the graveside and pulled something from inside of her coat. She placed the HORNETS' NEST T-shirt on the chest of the casket.

This action, while not inappropriate to the mourners, was inappropriate to her mother, who tactfully approached her daughter. Coach Laden stood. The team stood. Even Stacy Ann Sloan stood. Everyone waited for what would be next.

"What are you doing?" said her mother, removing the T-shirt from the casket. "This is your sister's funeral."

Fat Angie's head dropped, her chin doubling, her heartache tripling. Her eyes cut to the shirt dangling helplessly in her mother's hand. The magic of it squeezed out beneath her mother's grip.

"Please sit down," said her mother. "This is all almost over."

Over? No. No, no, she thought, with such precision, with such controlled understanding, that it frightened Fat Angie. She shook her head and stepped back. The sound of wet grass squeaked beneath her shoes. They were far too tight. Too new. Too not made for her.

"Angie!" Wang shouted, but she was already in full stride, leaping over grave markers and cutting between tombstones. The press pressing on her heels. For once, she did not care. Let them all see. Let them all gawk and analyze. Let them make up the truth of who she was.

She did not care.

She would run!

The day after the funeral Fat Angie stepped back into the gym, where her sister's joy of the game was immortalized behind the trophy-case glass.

Fat Angie knocked on Coach Laden's door.

"Hey, Angie," said Coach Laden, setting her paperwork down. "Have a seat."

Fat Angie shook her head and reached into a plastic grocery bag. She lay her sister's folded basketball jersey on Coach Laden's orderly desk.

"Thanks," said Fat Angie.

It was strange for Fat Angie to hear her voice aloud. The sound was different. She could not identify the difference right then.

"Why thanks?" asked Coach Laden.

"Just seemed like that's what I was supposed to say."

Coach Laden ran her hand over the jersey numbers.

"She begged for this number," Coach Laden said. "The jersey was too big. She didn't care. She just wanted this number. Forty-two. Does that seem like a lucky number?"

Fat Angie shrugged, her hand holding her other arm.

Coach Laden held the jersey out to Fat Angie. "You could always come back. Even if not now, next year."

Fat Angie shook her head.

"You remember what you said to me during tryouts?" Coach Laden asked. "You said you would follow through. That you wouldn't quit."

Fat Angie nodded, stuffing her hands into her hoodie pocket.

"You don't have to quit, Angie."

She backed away from Coach Laden's desk. "I'm . . ."

A deafening pang twisted in her not-so-plump gut. It raged and screamed and then muted. The mute sent a shiver — a distinct panic — down Fat Angie.

"Angie, just —"

But she dipped out of the office.

Fat Angie punched a wall and rushed out of the gymnasium, the image of her sister behind glass at her back.

Fat Angie continued to walk.

And walk.

Until her walk became a jog. A jog that became a sprint. Until she was gone.

A week after the funeral, Fat Angie had continued to run, pausing only for school, an hour and a half for meals, and six hours of sleep. Aside from that, she ran like Tom Hanks in Robert Zemeckis's multi-million dollar blockbuster *Forrest Gump.* Only Fat Angie ran the length of Dryfalls. From one place to the next to the next, forming a rather imperfect circle. If she could be seen from Google Earth, there would be a brown head with a plain white T-shirt traveling from city edge to city edge. But how often were such images updated, and what was the likelihood that she would be captured by their outer-atmosphere satellites? But in fact, she once was. In half stride.

The image appeared on CNN along with moment-to-moment coverage. When asked if she ran to stop the war, she said nothing. When asked if she ran for the loss of her sister, she said nothing. When asked anything, she said nothing.

In short, there was no comment.

At first, she mostly ran alone. Early before school and immediately thereafter. Even when she was seemingly stationary in her classrooms, she was running in her mind. Soon Jake and Ryan ran beside her. Ryan was distracted by the occasional hissing cat or red-chipped fire hydrant. He would gallop to their side after such distractions. The three became inseparable, but to Fat Angie, she ran alone.

December became January. Weeks and weeks had passed since her winning basket against the Tamblyn Titans. She had not spoken to anyone in class. She had not spoken to her mother or Wang in their super-tensed-up obligatory family meals. It seemed as though she wanted to live out her life as a cross-country running mute.

One evening, she slouched in the dark of her room. Her computer screen illuminated her desk in a pale blue-white, as it had every night since the funeral. The illegally downloaded YouTube video of her sister held hostage was on replay. How could she not see before? How could she not know that she had created a sister who was not in that video? Her sister was frightened. She was badly hurt. And if you looked closely into her eyes, the supersister Fat Angie knew on the basketball court of Dryfalls, Ohio, was gone. She was just a girl who knew she was about to die.

For the first time, tears streamed down Angie's face. The quiet cry broke into a deep, Earth-is-gonna-swallow-me cry. Her mother's reality—Wang's and Jake's reality—everyone's reality was now hers. Her sister was dead. She was never coming home.

"Hey . . ." The voice was faint.

Fat Angie was alone, beside her locker at William Anders High. The hallway was decimated. She climbed over the debris of bent metal and textbooks. Rain sprayed in from the gutted ceiling. Blinding white light punched through the windows. Loose-leaf paper leaped into the air. Fat Angie shuddered. Then—

Dribbling . . . a basketball—

"Angie." The voice became more distinct.

KC waited at the end of the hall. Her forearms exposed and scarless.

The dribbling grew louder . . .

A shutter clicked.

Fat Angie turned to—

"Wake up," said Wang.

Fat Angie robotically shifted her stiff body.

"You drooled on your keyboard," Wang said.

She squinted, orienting her eyes to the light of her room.

He closed out the window to the video that was still in loop on her computer. "It's six."

"So?" she said.

"So, isn't this when you run all Forrest Gump?"

"Huh?" she asked.

"Here." He threw a pair of sweatpants and sneakers at her. "I'll run with you today."

"Right," she said.

"Yo, I'm gonna do it," he said. "You coming or not?"

She kicked into the sweatpants, jammed into a hoodie, and they were off.

Down the stairs and past the framed photos of the former family perfectly posed. Fat Angie and Wang grabbed their house keys.

Jake stood in his driveway with Ryan at his side. He blew on his hands. "Hey," he said. "About time."

After a few quick stretches, they began to jog. Cutting past the Oaklawn Ends sign and through the sleeping streets.

It began to snow lightly. It had not snowed in Dryfalls all winter but there it was, fluttering down.

As they came up on Main Street, four runners in gray hoodies and sweatpants cut in behind them. Fat Angie crooked her head back. The four became eight. Then sixteen.

Boys and girls—basketball players from William Anders High. All with the number 42 pinned across their chests. Coach Laden and even Stacy Ann jogged among them. Though Stacy Ann's facial expression was a clear indicator she did not want to be there.

"What's going on?" Fat Angie asked Wang and Jake.

"Guess they just wanted to run," said Wang.

Fat Angie's heart raced.

"I don't get it," she said to Wang.

He shrugged. "Yeah, you do," he said.

The snow showered in sheets. The basketball players raised their hoodies' hoods almost in unison.

Fat Angie led the pack of runners as the town went from yawn to full awake. Dryfalls was abuzz with the sight. Snow sticking to the sidewalks, windshields, rooftops. Still they all ran. Together.

People lined the streets. They clapped. Some cheered. No numbers were chanted. No names. It was just a sound. A good one.

Then *she* walked through the crowd. Unmistakable as she had been on her first day in Fat Angie's gym class, KC Romance pushed through a pack of people to the street corner. Her cell in snapshot position fell to her side as the two girls locked looks. The longing . . . it was still there. Somewhere in the cadence of the running pack. Somewhere in the rocky history the two girls shared. Somewhere in the first snow in Dryfalls, Ohio, that year.

The girls . . . they longed.

The run completed approximately one hour later, back at Oaklawn Ends. Not all the team members finished. Some had hitched a ride in one of the many cars lining the cul-de-sac.

Coach Laden lovingly leaned in to Fat Angie and said, "Never quit." She gave the not-so-plump Angie her sister's basketball jersey. "Exceptional people just don't."

Coach Laden met up with the basketball teams. A few kids waved to Angie — not in a cruel way.

Wang collapsed against the garage. Jake threw his arm around Angie.

"You know, this won't change everything," she said.

"Yup," Jake said.

"Maybe it'll change me," she said.

"It's a little early for introspection," he said.

"Nice word," she said, mockingly. "Someone's been reading."

"Shut up," he said.

"Hey!" Wang said. "Let's eat, man. I'm wicked ten kinds of hungry, yo."

Wang led the way, opening the front door.

Their mother stood in her robe, espresso in hand.

"Shit," said Wang.

"Are you hungry?" asked Connie.

They suspiciously followed her into the kitchen.

"Jake, how's your mother?" said Angie's mom.

Jake poured orange juice from a pitcher. "Great."

"I guess you enjoyed your run," said her mother. "Amber Stevens said she saw you with the entire basketball squad. So you're back on the team?"

Angie set her sister's jersey on the marble countertop. "No."

Her couldn't-be-bothered mother acknowledged the jersey only with the slightest of pauses. But it was an acknowledgment nevertheless.

"Your color is off," said her mother.

"What?" Angie said. Her teeth cut into a Gala apple.

"All of this running," her mother continued. "I understand. . . . Actually, I don't.

"Anyway," said Angie's mother. "Bacon and eggs, Wang? Jake?"

"Lots of bacon," said Wang, mouth full of Frosted Flakes.

"What about me?" said Angie.

Connie braced herself against the refrigerator.

"Maybe I want breakfast," said Angie.

"I meant to include you," said her mother.

Angie shook her head. "No, you didn't."

"I did. Do you want—"

"All you see is fat," said Angie.

"Can you conceive that I just hadn't said your name yet?" asked her mother.

"It's not just breakfast," said Angie. "It's how you look at me. Or how you don't look at me."

Jake and Wang held out for what seemed to be quite the showdown.

"I'm looking at you, Angie. I'm watching you run all over CNN — "

"Because me running on CNN makes you look like what?" said Angie. "A heartless mother."

"Don't," her mother warned. "I'm just trying to have a civil exchange."

Her mother's eyes cut to Jake.

"What are you afraid of?" Angie asked. "That Jake might give an exclusive on how we continue to be screwed up?"

"You think I'm so shallow. You think I don't feel anything?"

"Not really," said Angie.

"I just accept that I have a life that goes beyond this one event."

"Event?" asked Angie. "Her death is not an event."

"Fine. Poor choice of words," said her mother. "That's the way it always is with you."

"Why can't you just say it?" Angie asked.

Her mother went back to the eggs and announced to everyone, "We'll all have breakfast."

"No," said Angie.

Her mother busied about the kitchen in an attempt to

deflect any potential for further discussion of her recently buried daughter. But Angie was not letting things slide any longer.

"You want me to be skinny. You want me to be normal. You want—"

"I want you to be happy," said her mother, cracking an egg with a chef's precision. "You and Wang. All of us."

"Happy?" said Angie, throwing the apple in the stainless steel garbage can.

Wang zipped his Tony Hawk lamb-lined hoodie and scratched his sweaty head.

"My sister is dead," said Angie. "They sent us a casket with *bones.* With pieces. You think making a breakfast will make us happy?"

Her mother dropped a shell piece in the bowl and desperately attempted to remove the bits of shell swimming in the slimy egg white. After several failed attempts, she stretched her neck, decided the shell bits would not affect the overall presentation of the breakfast, cracked another egg in the bowl.

"Mom, she's dead," said Angie.

"Jake, do you like scrambled eggs with cheese?" asked Angie's mother.

"Sure," Jake said.

"Listen to me!" said Angie.

Angie had unknowingly raised her voice. As a result she

had become the absolute center of attention in her mother's otherwise myopic world. Connie was, in fact, listening.

"You couldn't see her. You couldn't be bothered," said Angie. "You couldn't be bothered with *anything*! She didn't want to just save the world. She wanted *you* to see her. The *real* her. But your ideas—about what she had to be—the 'required steps of her future.' That's why she left us. That's why she left us all."

"Your sister made a choice, Angie."

Angie considered this thought. The idea of the choice. The veracity of it.

The silence. It was deafening until Jake twisted in his chair in what might be counted in mere increments. His sneaker, wet with snow, squeaked against the floor.

"You're kinda right," said Angie to her mother. "She made a choice. But she made that choice for you. And you know . . . at the funeral, all this time. All I could do was think how it was your fault. How you killed her because you just couldn't be bothered to see her. She's dead. Like really dead. And that's real, Mom. It's not an event. And I'm empty sometimes and I'm sad but mostly . . . I'm relieved."

"Relieved?" asked her mother. "Don't ever say that again."

"I am *relieved* she's not in some dark place, scared and thinking of all of us," said Angie.

Relieved. Angie was, in fact, absolutely and completely relieved. Until right then, she had had no idea. Not so much of an inkling. She had run. She had run because:

A. She enjoyed the intensity of forward motion
B. Said forward motion gave her freedom
C. She was guilty about feeling relief

The word fit. It was the perfect size. And that was OK.

The doorbell rang.

It was one of those moments of not knowing who should move first.

"I'll just go . . . to the door," Jake said, stepping behind Angie.

"Are you finished?" asked her mother.

Angie shook her head. "I don't know what it takes."

"What does that mean?" asked her mother.

"Angie," Jake called from the front door.

"You shouldn't have to ask." Angie headed down the hall.

"Angie," said her mother. "I am not cold. I am not narrow."

Angie considered her mother's statement for 3.2 seconds. Then walked to the door.

Jake stepped aside. KC Romance stood on the welcome mat.

"Hey," said KC, her purple heart tattoo extra beautiful somehow.

Angie was not pleased to see her. Not in any way that could be clocked.

"I think this is the part where I go home," Jake said.

"Stay," said Angie.

"Text me," he said.

Jake jogged across the street.

"You OK?" asked KC.

"Yeah," said Angie.

KC shook off a shiver. Her breath cloud puffed and faded between breaths.

"I've seen you around town," said KC, shivering in the cold.

"I run."

"Yeah, I've seen — saw," said KC. "That was something this morning. You running."

"I guess."

That awkward space that finds its way into most lives had found its home between the girls. It was that sad awkward that didn't know what do to with itself.

"What do you want?" said Angie.

KC nodded, the toe of her right combat boot tipping up. "Guess I'm a little late to the 'I'm sorry,' huh?" asked KC.

Angie was no longer one for revealing cards.

"But I am — sorry," said KC. "About what I said to

you — what I called you that day at my house. It was all melted-crazed — my dad and me. I didn't — "

"It doesn't matter," said Angie.

Unbelievable heavy pause.

"Yeah, but it does," said KC. "I was at the funeral."

Angie nodded.

"I just kinda hung back. Behind a camera crew. I left flowers after. On top of the T-shirt."

"What?"

"The one you were always wearing. Your mom put it on the casket after you took off."

All of the running. All of the anger.

Angie had not remembered the T-shirt moment until that moment.

She had never thought to ask where it had gone.

Her mother was not frozen. Not in any absolute sense. The reality of the thought had caught Angie very much off-guard.

"Anyway, I just wanted — "

"Well, thanks for the flowers," said Angie, closing the door.

In dramatic fashion, KC jammed her boot between the door and the frame.

"Let me SparkNote it," said KC.

"I'm not much into the abbreviated truth," said Angie.

"Yeah, I know," said KC. "The thing is . . . you saw me as cool and beautiful and . . . kind of on the rebel side."

"No," said Angie.

"Yeah, you did."

"I saw you as my friend," said Angie.

"I am your friend," said KC. "But friends screw up, Angie. They have flaws. It was a shit day. And no one's ever walked in on the whole slice and dice—"

"Cutting."

"Yeah, cutting," said KC. "It's kind of a private thing. I freaked." KC's boot toe turned upward again. "Look, I was ashamed that you busted in—that you saw. Plus, I was just—"

"Free fallin'?"

"Kinda," KC said. "And I lied. I wasn't over the whole cutting. Angie, it's just . . . It's so hard when the person you look like on the outside doesn't really match how you feel on the inside. You know?"

Angie nodded. She did, in fact, know.

"Anyway, Esther's got me in with some twelve-year-old shrink with more degrees than a freakin' thermometer," said KC.

"That's, um . . . that's good."

KC heaved one of those rather enormous breaths.

"It is, actually."

KC drew a miniheart in the snow with the toe of her boot.

"Well, I guess . . ." said Angie.

"I messed up."

"Yeah," Angie said.

"Really bad," KC continued.

"Yeah."

"I miss you," said KC.

Pause.

Dramatic movie-like pause.

KC's hand reached into her hoodie pocket and emerged with a closed fist. Angie, functioning on Angie processing time, took a moment to realize she should open her hand.

"It's for you," said KC.

The crackle of plastic was the first sound before KC pulled her hand away from Angie's. It was a Japanese-imported light-up candy ring.

"I hope you like watermelon-kiwi-banana. That's all they had. I mean, I asked. They had, like, three cases in the back of the same kind."

Angie's shoulders relaxed. Her entire body felt less rigid.

"It's my favorite," said Angie.

KC bit her lower lip and reached into her messenger bag. "Here. I read it."

The joy of the candy ring faded. Angie took the crumpled envelope.

"I think you should mail it," KC said.

"My sister's dead, KC," said Angie.

"That doesn't mean you can't mail it."

"Thanks," said Angie.

"For?" asked KC.

"The Japanese-imported light-up candy ring."

"Yeah," said KC. "I mean . . . yeah."

"I gotta . . ." said Angie.

"Yeah, I was — I should. Leave," said KC.

"Look, this. You and me," said Angie. "It's like you said. It's complicated."

"Hmm." KC nodded and then began doing what the neighbors would later call quite unusual.

She belted out a song that mashed the wickedness of pop rebel Pink with the nostalgia of Patsy Cline, *"Heard you'd been feeling kinda low . . ."*

"KC . . ." Angie said.

KC continued singing, pulling Angie out into the falling snow.

"Been thinking 'bout me but just don't know
How to reach out
Will I return the call
Wondering if you really know me at all . . .

Here's the note
I shoulda passed in class
Can't stop thinkin'
'Bout how you make me feel at last . . .

So raise your voice
Make it heard

Hold my hand
'Cause I'm the one who always understood . . .
I'm the one who understands
That sweet freaky lil' heart
Resting in the palm of my hand . . ."

The very high-octane teen-drama moment seemed too well scripted for the life of Angie. But there she was. Standing in such a moment with KC Romance, snow falling all around them. Interestingly enough, she did not feel an urge to pee.

"Angie, everything's complicated. Look, you really want me to go — be gone. I will." KC dug through her messenger bag. "But while I pay ample lip service to my frustration with the capitalistic system that is America, I got this for you."

Angie held the thinly wrapped item with the signature KC Romance heart on the front. Only the signature heart was red, not purple.

"It was for Christmas but it didn't seem like the right time," KC said.

With a few quick movements, Fat Angie had opened . . .

"The *Freaks and Geeks Yearbook Edition,"* Angie said.

"It's used, but *gently* used," said KC.

"It's the best gift ever. I mean, besides the Japanese-imported light-up candy ring."

"Yeah?"

"Yeah," said Angie.

"So . . . maybe you wanna marathon? We got some great soy nog at the house," said KC. "It's Esther's specialty."

Angie considered this offer for quite a long time. For . . . exactly 3.5 seconds, give or take a second for good measure.

"OK," Angie said.

"OK," KC said, her smile ultra-electric.

Angie stopped at the mailbox and slid the letter to her sister inside. She lifted the flag.

She took KC's hand. Smilefest revved at full throttle as they stepped off the snowy curb.

"I wonder what happens next," said KC.

Angie grinned. "I don't know."

The two girls neared the end of the cul-de-sac, turned the corner, and . . .

There was a girl. Her name was Angie. She was happy.

ACKNOWLEDGMENTS

Amazing thanks . . .
to my insightful, fantastic agent, Andrea Cascardi, and to my inspiring editor, Joan Powers. And thank you to my friends and colleagues: Josh Flowers, C.G. Watson, Howard Wells III, Karl Miller, Andrew J. Brown, Esme Codell, Sondra McClendon, Sally Derby, Galen Todd McGriff, Sara St. Martin-Lynne, Leslie Gallagher, Amanda Cunningham, Patrick Zapata, Stephanie Schiro, Abigail Sanders-Wells, Margaret Coble, Tina Tramel Zapata, Matthew Gallagher, S.E. Miller, Anouck Van Troy-Struyf, Betty Thomas, Amber Nash, Jordan Neff, my fantastic brother Kurt Struyf, and Joss Whedon for inspiring me to write strong female characters!

Absolute Special Thanks . . .
To Linda Sanders-Wells for recognizing my potential as a writer, filmmaker, and human being; and Shirley Klock for your kindness, quirkiness, and love for *Fat Angie.*